1 MONTH OF FREE READING

at

www.ForgottenBooks.com

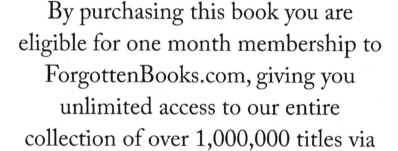

By purchasing this book you are eligible for one month membership to ForgottenBooks.com, giving you unlimited access to our entire collection of over 1,000,000 titles via our web site and mobile apps.

To claim your free month visit:
www.forgottenbooks.com/free35939

* Offer is valid for 45 days from date of purchase. Terms and conditions apply.

ISBN 978-0-483-12063-1
PIBN 10035939

This book is a reproduction of an important historical work. Forgotten Books uses
state-of-the-art technology to digitally reconstruct the work, preserving the original format
whilst repairing imperfections present in the aged copy. In rare cases, an imperfection in
the original, such as a blemish or missing page, may be replicated in our edition. We do,
however, repair the vast majority of imperfections successfully; any imperfections that
remain are intentionally left to preserve the state of such historical works.

Forgotten Books is a registered trademark of FB &c Ltd.
Copyright © 2018 FB &c Ltd.
FB &c Ltd, Dalton House, 60 Windsor Avenue, London, SW19 2RR.
Company number 08720141. Registered in England and Wales.

For support please visit www.forgottenbooks.com

STUDIES IN LOVE
AND IN TERROR

BY
MRS. BELLOC LOWNDES

NEW YORK
CHARLES SCRIBNER'S SONS
1913

HARVARD COLLEGE LIBRARY
BEQUEST OF
WINWARD PRESCOTT
JANUARY 27, 1933

CONTENTS

	PAGE
PRICE OF ADMIRALTY	1
THE CHILD	99
ST. CATHERINE'S EVE	131
THE WOMAN FROM PURGATORY	187
WHY THEY MARRIED	227

STUDIES IN LOVE
AND IN TERROR

PRICE OF ADMIRALTY

PRICE OF ADMIRALTY

"O mort, vieux capitaine, il est temps ! levons l'ancre !
Ce pays nous ennuie, O mort ! Appareillons ! "

I

CLAIRE DE WISSANT, wife of Jacques de Wissant, Mayor of Falaise, stood in the morning sunlight, graceful with a proud, instinctive grace of poise and gesture, on a wind-blown path close to the edge of the cliff.

At some little distance to her left rose the sloping, mansard roofs of the Pavillon de Wissant, the charming country house to which her husband had brought her, a seventeen year old bride, ten long years ago.

She was now gazing eagerly out to sea, shielding her grey, heavy-lidded eyes with her right hand. From her left hand hung a steel chain, to which was attached a small key.

A hot haze lay heavily over the great sweep of deep blue waters. It blotted out the low grey line on the horizon which, on the majority of each year's days, reminds the citizens of Falaise how near England is to France.

Jacques de Wissant had rejoiced in the *entente cordiale*, if only because it brought such a stream of tourists to the old seaport town of which he was now Mayor. But his beautiful wife thought of the English as gallant foes rather than as friends. Was she not great-granddaughter to that admiral who at Trafalgar, when both his legs were shattered by chain-shot, bade his men place him in a barrel of bran that he might go on commanding, in the hour of defeat, to the end?

And yet as Claire stood there, her eyes sweeping the sea for an as yet invisible craft, her heart seemed to beat rhythmically to the last verse of a noble English poem which the governess of her twin daughters had made them recite to her that very morning. How did it run? Aloud she murmured:

> "Yet this inconstancy is such,
> As you too shall adore—"

and then she stopped, her quivering lips refusing to form the two concluding lines.

To Claire de Wissant, that moving cry from a man's soul was not dulled by familiarity, or hackneyed by common usage, and just now it found an intolerably faithful echo in her sad, rebellious heart, intensifying the anguish born of a secret and very bitter renunciation.

With an abrupt, restless movement she turned and walked on till her way along the path was barred by a curious obstacle. This was a small red-brick tower, built within a few feet of the edge of the cliff. It was an ugly blot on the beautiful stretch of down, all the uglier that the bricks and tiles had not yet had time to lose their hardness of line and colour in the salt wind.

On the cliff side, the small circular building, open to wind, sky and sea, formed the unnatural apex of a natural stairway which led steeply, almost vertically, down to a deep land-locked cove below. The irregular steps carved by nature out of the chalk had been strengthened, and a rough protection added by means of knotted ropes fixed on either side of the dangerous descent.

In the days when the steps had started sheer from a cleft in the cliff path, Jacques de Wissant had never used this way of reaching a spot which till last year had been his property, and his favourite bathing-place; and he had also, in those same quiet days which now seemed so long ago, forbidden his daughters to use that giddy way. But Claire was a fearless woman; and she had always preferred the dangerous, ladder-like stairs which seemed, when gazed at from below, to hang 'twixt sky and sea.

Now, however, she rarely availed herself of the right retained by her husband of using one of the two keys which unlocked the door set in the new brick tower, for the cove—only by courtesy could it be called a bay—had been chosen, owing to its peculiar position, naturally remote and yet close to a great maritime port, to be the quarters of the Northern Submarine Flotilla.

Jacques de Wissant—and it was perhaps the only time in their joint life that his wife had entirely understood and sympathized with any action of her husband's—had refused the compensation his Government had offered him; more, in his cold, silent way, he had shown himself a patriot in a sense comparatively few modern men have the courage to be, namely, in that which affected both his personal comfort and his purse.

After standing for a moment on the perilously small and narrow platform which made the floor of the tower, Claire grasped firmly a strand of the knotted rope and began descending the long steps cut in the cliff side. She no longer gazed out to sea, instead she looked straight down into the pale green, sun-flecked waters of the little bay, where seven out of the nine submarines which composed the flotilla were lying half-submerged, as is their wont in harbour.

A landsman, coming suddenly upon the cliff-locked pool, might have thought that the centuries had rolled back, and that the strange sight before him was a school of saurians lazily sunning themselves in the placid waters of a sea inlet where time had stood still.

But no such vision came to Claire de Wissant. As she went down the cliff-side her lovely eyes rested on these sinister, man-created monsters with a feeling of sisterly, possessive affection. She had become so familiarly acquainted with each and all of them in the last few months; she knew with such a curious, intimate knowledge where they differed, both from each other and also from other submarine craft, not only here, in these familiar waters, but in the waters of France's great rival on the sea. . . .

It ever gave her a thrill of pride to remember that it was France which first led the way in this, the most dangerous as also the most adventurous new arm of naval warfare: and she rejoiced as fiercely, as exultantly as any of her sea-fighting forbears would have done in the terrible potentialities of destruction which each of these strange, grotesque-looking craft bore in their narrow flanks.

It was now the hour of the crews' midday meal; there were fewer men standing about than usual; and so, after she had stepped down on the sandy strip of shore, and climbed the ladder leading to the old Napoleonic hulk which served as workshop and dwelling-place of the officers of the flotilla, Madame de Wissant for a few moments stood solitary, and looked musingly down into the waters of the bay.

Each submarine, its long, fish-like shape lying prone in the almost still, transparent water, differed not only in size, but in make, from its fellows, and no two conning towers even were alike.

Lying apart, as if sulking in a corner, was an example of the old "Gymnote" type of under-sea boat. She went by the name of the *Carp*, and she was very squat, small and ugly, her telescopic conning tower being of hard canvas.

To Claire, the *Carp* always recalled an old Breton woman she had known as a girl. That woman had given thirteen sons to France, and of the thirteen five had died while serving with the colours—three at sea and two in Tonkin—

and a grateful country had given her a pension of ten francs a week, two francs for each dead son.

Like that Breton woman, the ugly, sturdy little *Carp* had borne heroes in her womb, and like her, too, she had paid terrible toll of her sons to death.

Occasionally, but very seldom now, the *Carp* was taken out to sea, and the men, strange to say, liked being in her, for they regarded her as a lucky boat; she had never had what they called a serious accident.

Sunk deeper in the water was the broad-backed *Abeille*, significantly named "La Pétroleuse," the heroine of four explosions, no favourite with either crews or commanders; and, cradled in a low dock on the farther strip of beach, was stretched the *Triton*, looking like a huge fish which had panted itself to death. The *Triton* also was not a lucky boat; she had been the theatre of a terrible mishap when, for some inexplicable cause, the conning tower had failed to close. Claire was always glad to see her safe in dock.

Out in the middle of the bay was *La Glorieuse*, a submarine of the latest type. Had she not lain so low, little more than her flying bridge being above the water, she would have put her elder sisters to shame, so exquisitely shaped was she. Everything about *La Glorieuse* was made delicately true to scale, and she could carry a crew of over twenty men. But somehow Claire de Wissant did not care for this miniature leviathan as she did for the older kind of submarine, and, with more reason for his prejudice, the officer in charge of the flotilla shared her feeling. Commander Dupré thought *La Glorieuse* difficult to handle under water. But he had had the same opinion of the *Neptune*, one of the two submarines which were out this fine August morning. . . .

An eager "Bonjour, madame," suddenly sounded in Claire de Wissant's ear, and she turned quickly to find one of the younger officers at her elbow.

"The *Neptune* is a few minutes late," he said smiling. "I hope your sister has enjoyed her cruise!" He was looking with admiring and grateful eyes at the young wife of the Mayor of Falaise, for Claire de Wissant and her widowed sister, Madeleine Baudoin, were very kind and hospitable to the officers of the submarine flotilla.

The life of both officers and men who volunteer for this branch of the service is grim and arduous. And if this is generally true of them all, it was specially so of those who served under Commander Dupré. By a tacit agreement with their chief, they took no part in the summer gaieties of the watering-place which has grown up round the old port of Falaise, and out of duty hours they would have led dull lives indeed had it not been for the hospitality shown them by the owners of the Pavillon de Wissant, and for the welcome which awaited them in the freer, gayer atmosphere of Madame Baudoin's villa, the Châlet des Dunes.

Madeleine Baudoin was a lively, cheerful woman, younger in nature if not in years than her beautiful sister, and so she was naturally more popular with the younger officers. They had felt especially flattered when Madame Baudoin had allowed herself to be persuaded to go out for a couple of hours in the *Neptune;* till this morning neither of the sisters had ever ventured out to sea in a submarine.

And now 'twas true that the *Neptune* had been out longer than her commander had said she would be, but no touch of fear brushed Claire de Wissant; she would have trusted what she held most precious in the world—her children—to Commander Dupré's care, and a few moments after her companion had spoken she suddenly saw the little tricolor, for which her keen eyes had for long swept the sea, bravely riding the waves, and making straight for the bay.

The flag moving swiftly over the surface of the blue water was a curious, almost an uncanny sight; one which never failed to fill Claire with a kind of spiritual exaltation. For the tiny strip of waving colour was a symbol of the gallantry, of the carelessness of danger, lying under the dancing, sun-flecked ripples which alone proved that the tricolor was not some illusion of sorcery.

And then, as if the submarine had been indeed a sentient, living thing, the *Neptune* lifted her great shield-like back up out of the sea and glided through the narrow neck of the bay, and so close under the long deck on which Madame de Wissant and her companion were standing.

The eager, busy hum of work slackened—discipline is not perhaps quite so taut in the French as it is in the British Navy—for both men and officers were one and all eager to see the lady who had ventured out in the *Neptune* with their commander. Only those actually on board had seen Madame Baudoin embark; there was a long, rough jetty close to her house, the lonely Châlet des Dunes, and it was from there the submarine had picked up her honoured passenger.

But when Commander Dupré's stern, sunburnt face suddenly appeared above the conning tower, the men vanished as if by enchantment, while the eager, busy hum began again, much as if a lever, setting this human machinery in motion, had been touched by some titanic finger.

The officers naturally held their ground.

There was a look of strain in the Commander's blue eyes, and his mouth was set in hard lines; a thoughtful onlooker would have suspected that the exciting, dangerous life he led was trying his nerves. His men knew better; still, though they had no clue to the cause which had changed him, they all knew he had changed greatly of late; to them individually he had become kinder, more human, and that heightened their regret that he was now quitting the Northern Flotilla.

Commander Dupré had asked to be transferred to the Toulon Submarine Station; some experiments were being made there which he was anxious to watch. He was leaving Falaise on the morrow.

Claire de Wissant reddened, and a gleam leapt into her eyes as she met the naval officer's grave, measuring glance. But very soon he looked away from her, for now he was bending down, putting out a hand to help his late passenger to step from the conning tower.

Smiling, breathless, a little dishevelled, her grey linen skirt crumpled, Madame Baudoin looked round her, dazed for the moment by the bright sunlight. Then she called out gaily:

"Well, Claire! Here I am—alive and very, very hot!"

And as she jumped off the slippery flank of the *Neptune*, she gave herself and her crumpled gown a little shake, and made a slight, playful grimace.

The bright young faces round her broke into broad grins—those officers who volunteer for the submarine services of the world are chosen young, and they are merry boys.

"You may well laugh, messieurs,"—she threw them all a lively challenging glance—"when I tell you that to-day, for the first time in my life, I acknowledge masculine supremacy! I think that you will admit that we women are not afraid of pain, but the discomfort, the—the stuffiness? Ah, no—I could not have borne much longer the horrible discomfort and stuffiness of that dreadful little *Neptune* of yours!"

Protesting voices rose on every side. The *Neptune* was not uncomfortable! The *Neptune* was not stuffy!

"And I understand"—again she made a little grimace—"that it is quite an exceptional thing for the crew to be consoled, as I was today, by an ice-pail!"

"A most exceptional thing," said the youngest lieutenant, with a sigh. His name was Paritot, and he also had been out with the *Neptune* that morning. "In fact, it only happens in that week which sees four Thursdays—or when we have a lady on board, madame!"

"What a pity it is," said another, "that the old woman who left a legacy to the inventor who devises a submarine life-saving apparatus didn't leave us instead a cream-ice allowance! It would have been a far more practical thing to do."

Madame Baudoin turned quickly to Commander Dupré, who now stood silent, smileless, at her sister's side.

"Surely you're going to try for this extraordinary prize?" she cried. "I'm sure that you could easily devise something which would gain the old lady's legacy."

"I, madame?" he answered with a start, almost as if he were wrenching himself free from some deep abstraction. "I should not think of trying to do such a thing! It would be a mere waste of time. Besides, there is no real risk—no risk that we are not prepared to run." He looked proudly round at the eager, laughing faces of the youngsters who were, till to-morrow night, still under his orders.

"The old lady meant very well," he went on, and for the first time since he had stepped out of the conning tower Commander Dupré smiled. "And I hope with all my heart that some poor devil will get her money! But I think I may promise you that it will not be an officer in the submarine service. We are too busy, we have too many really important things to do, to worry ourselves about life-saving appliances. Why, the first thing we should do if pressed for room would be to throw our life-helmets overboard!"

"Has one of the life-helmets ever saved a life?"

It was Claire who asked the question in her low, vibrating voice.

Commander Dupré turned to her, and he flushed under his sunburn. It was the first time she had spoken to him that day.

"No, never," he answered shortly. And then, after a pause, he added, "the conditions in which these life-helmets could be utilized only occur in one accident in a thousand——"

"Still, they would have saved our comrades in the *Lutin*," objected Lieutenant Paritot.

The *Lutin?* There was a moment's silence.

The evocation of that tricksy sprite, the Ariel of French mythology, whose name, by an ironical chance, had been borne by the most ill-fated of all submarine craft, seemed to bring the shadow of death athwart them all.

Madeleine Baudoin felt a sudden tremor of retrospective fear. She was glad she had not remembered the *Lutin* when she was sitting, eating ices, and exchanging frivolous, chaffing talk with Lieutenant Paritot in that chamber of little ease, the drum-like interior of the *Neptune*, where not even she, a small woman, could stand upright.

"Well, well! We must not keep you from your *déjeuner!*" she cried, shaking off the queer, disturbing sensation. "I have to thank you for—shall I say a very interesting experience? I am too honest to say an agreeable one!"

She shook hands with Commander Dupré and Lieutenant Paritot, the officers who had accompanied her on what had been, now that she looked back on it, perhaps a more perilous adventure than she had realized.

"You're coming with me, Claire?" She looked at her sister—it was a tender, anxious, loving look; Madeleine Baudoin had been the eldest, and Claire de Wissant the youngest, of a Breton admiral's family of three daughters and four sons; they two were devoted to one another.

Claire shook her head. "I came to tell you that I can't lunch with you to-day," she said slowly. "I promised I would be back by half-past twelve."

"Then we shall not meet till to-morrow?"

Claire repeated mechanically, "No, not till to-morrow, dear Madeleine."

"May I row you home, madame?" Lieutenant Paritot asked Madeleine eagerly.

"Certainly, *mon ami*."

And so, a very few minutes later, Claire de Wissant and Commander Dupré were left alone together—alone, that is, save for fifty inquisitive, if kindly, pairs of eyes which saw them from every part of the bay.

At last she held out her hand. "Good-bye, then, till to-morrow," she said, her voice so low as to be almost inaudible.

"No, not good-bye yet!" he cried imperiously. "You must let me take you up the cliff to-day. It may be—I suppose it is—the last time I shall be able to do so."

Hardly waiting for her murmured word of assent, he led the way up the steep, ladder-like stairway cut in the cliff side; half-way up there were some very long steps, and it was from above that help could best be given. He longed with a fierce, aching longing that she would allow him to take her two hands in his and draw her up those high, precipitous steps. But of late Claire had avoided accepting from him, her friend, this simple, trifling act of courtesy. And now twice he turned and held out a hand, and twice she pretended not to see it.

At last, within ten feet of the top of the cliff, they came to the steepest, rudest step of all—a place some might have thought very dangerous.

Commander Dupré bent down and looked into Claire's uplifted face. "Let me at least help you up here," he said hoarsely.

She shook her head obstinately—but suddenly he felt her tremulous lips touch his lean, sinewy hand, and her hot tears fall upon his fingers.

He gave a strangled cry of pain and of pride, of agony and of rapture, and for a long moment he battled with an awful temptation. How easy it would be to gather her into his arms, and, with her face hidden on his breast, take a great leap backwards into nothingness. . . .

But he conquered the persuasive devil who had been raised—women do not know how easy it is to rouse this devil—by Claire's moment of piteous self-revelation.

And at last they stood together on the narrow platform where she, less than an hour ago, had stood alone.

Sheltered by the friendly, ugly red walls of the little tower, they were as remote from their kind as if on a rock in the midst of the sea. More, she was in his power in a sense she had never been before, for she had herself broken down the fragile barrier with which she had hitherto known how to keep him at bay. But he felt rather than saw that it was herself she would despise if now, at the eleventh hour, he took advantage of that tremulous kiss of renunciation, of those hot tears of anguished parting—and so—"Then at eleven o'clock to-morrow morning?" he said, and he felt as if it was some other man, not he himself, who was saying the words. He took her hand in farewell—so much he could allow himself—and all unknowing crushed her fingers in his strong, convulsive grasp.

"Yes," she said, "at eleven to-morrow morning Madeleine and I will be waiting out on the end of the jetty."

He thought he detected a certain hesitancy in her voice.

"Are you sure you still wish to come?" he said gravely. "I would not wish you to do anything that would cause you any fear—or any discomfort. Your sister evidently found it a very trying experience to-day——"

Claire smiled. Her hand no longer hurt her; her fingers had become quite numb.

"Afraid?" she said, and there was a little scorn in her voice. And then, "Ah me! I only wish that there were far more risk than there is about that which we are going to do together to-morrow." She was in a dangerous mood, poor soul—the mood that raises a devil in men. But perhaps her good angel came to help her, for suddenly, "Forgive me," she said humbly. "You know I did not mean that! Only cowards wish for death."

And then, looking at him, she averted her eyes, for they showed her that, if that were so, Dupré was indeed a craven.

"*Au revoir*," she whispered; "*au revoir* till to-morrow morning."

When half-way through the door, leading on to the lonely stretch of down, she turned round suddenly. "I do not want you to bring any ices for me to-morrow."

"I never thought of doing so," he said simply. And the words pleased Claire as much as anything just then could pleasure her, for they proved that her friend did not class her in his mind with those women who fear discomfort more than danger.

It had been her own wish to go out with Commander Dupré for his last cruise in northern waters. She had not had the courage to deny herself this final glimpse of him—they were never to meet again after to-morrow—in his daily habit as he lived.

II

At nine o'clock the next morning Jacques de Wissant stood in his wife's boudoir.

It was a strange and beautiful room, likely to linger in the memory of those who knew its strange and beautiful mistress.

The walls were draped with old Persian shawls, the furniture was of red Chinese lacquer, a set acquired in the East by some Norman sailing man unnumbered years ago, and bought by Claire de Wissant out of her own slender income not long after her marriage.

Pale blue and faded yellow silk cushions softened the formal angularity of the wide cane-seated couch and low, square chairs. There was a deep crystal bowl of midsummer flowering roses on the table, laden with books, by which Claire often sat long hours reading poetry and volumes written by modern poets and authors of whom her husband had only vaguely heard and of whom he definitely disapproved.

The window was wide open, and there floated in from the garden, which sloped away to the edge and indeed over the crumbling cliff, fragrant, salt-laden odours, dominated by the clean, sharp scent thrown from huge shrubs of red and white geraniums. The balls of blossom set against the belt of blue sea, formed a band of waving tricolor.

But Jacques de Wissant was unconscious, uncaring of the beauty round him, either in the room or without, and when at last he walked forward to the window, his face hardened as his eyes instinctively sought out the spot where, if hidden from his sight, he knew there lay the deep transparent waters of the little bay which had been selected as providing ideal quarters for the submarine flotilla.

He had eagerly assented to the sacrifice of his land, and, what meant far more to him, of his privacy; but now he would have given much—and he was a careful man—to have had the submarine station swept away, transferred to the other side of Falaise.

Down there, out of sight of the Pavillon, and yet but a few minutes away (if one used the dangerous cliff-stairway), dwelt Jacques de Wissant's secret foe, for the man of whom he was acutely, miserably jealous was Commander Dupré, of whose coming departure he as yet knew nothing.

The owner of the Pavillon de Wissant seldom entered the room where he now stood impatiently waiting for his wife, and he never did so without looking round him with distaste, and remembering with an odd, wistful feeling what it had been like in his mother's time. Then "le boudoir de madame" had reflected the tastes and simple interests of an old-fashioned provincial lady born in the year that Louis Philippe came to the throne. Greatly did the man now standing there prefer the room as it had been to what it was now!

The heavy, ugly furniture which had been there in the days of his lonely youth, for he had been an only child, was now in the schoolroom where the twin daughters of the house, Clairette and Jacqueline, did their lessons with Miss Doughty, their English governess.

Clairette and Jacqueline? Jacques de Wissant's lantern-jawed, expressionless face quickened into feeling as he thought of his two little girls. They were the pride, as well as the only vivid pleasure, of his life. All that he dispassionately admired in his wife was, so he sometimes told himself with satisfaction, repeated in his daughters. Clairette and Jacqueline had inherited their mother's look of race, her fastidiousness and refinement of bearing, while fortunately lacking Claire's dangerous personal beauty, her touch of eccentricity, and her discontent with life—or rather with the life which Jacques de Wissant, in spite of a gnawing ache and longing that nothing could still or assuage, yet found good.

The Mayor of Falaise looked strangely out of keeping with his present surroundings, at least so he would have seemed to the eye of any foreigner, especially of any Englishman, who had seen him standing there.

He was a narrowly built man, forty-three years of age, and his clean-shaven, rather fleshy face was very pale. On this hot August morning he was dressed in a light grey frock-coat, under which he wore a yellow waistcoat, and on his wife's writing-table lay his tall hat and lemon-coloured gloves.

As mayor of his native town—a position he owed to an historic name and to his wealth, and not to his very moderate Republican opinions—his duties included the celebration of civil marriages, and to-day, it being the 14th of August, the eve of the Assumption, and still a French national fête, there were to be a great many weddings celebrated in the Hôtel de Ville.

Jacques de Wissant considered that he owed it to himself, as well as to his fellow-citizens, to appear "correctly" attired on such occasions. He had a deep, wordless contempt for those of his acquaintances who dressed on ceremonial occasions "à l'anglaise," that is, in loose lounge suits and straw hats.

Suddenly there broke on his ear the sound of a low, full voice, singing. It came from the next room, his wife's bedroom, and the mournful passionate words of an old sea ballad rang out, full of a desolate pain and sense of bitter loss.

The sound irritated him shrewdly, and there came back to him a fragment of conversation he had not thought of for ten years. During a discussion held between his father and mother in this very room about their adored only son's proposed marriage with Claire de Kergouët, his father had said: "There is one thing I do not much care for; she is, they say, very musical, and Jacques, even as a baby, howled like a dog whenever he heard singing!" And his mother had laughed, "*Mon ami*, you cannot expect to get perfection, even for our Jacques!" And Claire, so he now admitted unwillingly to himself, had never troubled him overmuch with her love of music. . . .

He knocked twice, sharply, on his wife's door.

The song broke short with an almost cruel suddenness, and yet there followed a perceptible pause before he heard her say, "Come in."

And then, as Jacques de Wissant slowly turned the handle of the door, he saw his wife, Claire, before she saw him. He had a vision, that is, of her as she appeared when she believed herself to be, if not alone, then in sight of eyes that were indifferent, unwatchful. But Jacques' eyes, which his wife's widowed sister, the frivolous Parisienne, Madeleine Baudoin, had once unkindly compared to fishes' eyes, were now filled with a watchful, suspicious light which gave a tragic mask to his pallid, plain-featured face.

Claire de Wissant was standing before a long, narrow mirror placed at right angles to a window looking straight out to sea. Her short, narrow, dark blue skirt and long blue silk jersey silhouetted her slender figure, the figure which remained so supple, so—so girlish, in spite of her nine-year-old daughters. There was something shy and wild, untamed and yet beckoning, in the oval face now drawn with pain and sleeplessness, in the grey, almond-shaped eyes reddened with secret tears, and in the firm, delicately modelled mouth.

She was engaged in tucking up her dark, curling hair under a grey yachting cap, and, for a few moments, she neither spoke nor looked round to see who was standing framed in the door. But when, at last, she turned away from the mirror and saw her husband, the colour, rushing into her pale face, caused an unbecoming flush to cover it.

"I thought it was one of the children," she said, a little breathlessly. And then she waited, assuming, or so Jacques thought, an air at once of patience and of surprise which sharply angered him.

Then her look of strain, nay, of positive illness, gave him an uneasy twinge of discomfort. Could it be anxiety concerning her second sister, Marie-Anne, who, married to an Italian officer, was now ill of scarlet fever at Mantua? Two days ago Claire had begged very earnestly to be allowed to go and nurse Marie-Anne. But he, Jacques, had refused, not unkindly, but quite firmly. Claire's duty of course lay at Falaise, with her husband and children; not at Mantua, with her sister.

Suddenly she again broke silence. "Well?"

she said. "Is there anything you wish to tell me?" They had never used the familiar "thee" and "thou" the one to the other, for at the time of their marriage an absurd whim of fashion had ordained on the part of French wives and husbands a return to eighteenth-century formality, and Claire had chosen, in that one instance, to follow fashion.

She added, seeing that he still did not speak, "I am lunching with my sister to-day, but I shall be home by three o'clock." She spoke with the chill civility a lady shows a stranger. Claire seldom allowed herself to be on the defensive when speaking to her husband.

Jacques de Wissant frowned. He did not like either of his wife's sisters, neither the one who was now lying ill in Italy, nor his widowed sister-in-law, Madeleine Baudoin. In the villa which she had hired for the summer, and which stood on a lonely stretch of beach beyond the bay, Madeleine often entertained the officers of the submarine flotilla, and this, from her brother-in-law's point of view, was very far from "correct" conduct on the part of one who could still pass as a young widow.

In response to his frown there had come a slight, mocking smile on Claire's face.

"I suppose you are on your way to some important town function?"

She disliked the town of Falaise, the townfolk bored her, and she hated the vast old family house in the Market Place, where she had to spend each winter.

"To-day is the fourteenth of August," observed Jacques de Wissant in his deliberate voice; "and I have a great many marriages to celebrate this morning."

"Yes, I suppose that is so." And again Claire de Wissant spoke with the courteous indifference, the lack of interest in her husband's concerns, which she had early schooled him to endure.

But all at once there came a change in her voice, in her manner. "Why to-day—the fourteenth of August—is our wedding day! How stupid of me to forget! We must tell Jacqueline and Clairette. It will amuse them——"

She uttered the words a little breathlessly, and as she spoke, Jacques de Wissant walked quickly forward into the room. As he did so his wife moved abruptly away from where she had been standing, thus maintaining the distance between them.

But Claire de Wissant need not have been afraid; her husband had his own strict code of manners, and to this code he ever remained faithful. He possessed a remarkable mastery of his emotions, and he had always showed with regard to herself so singular a power of self-restraint that Claire, not unreasonably, doubted if he had any emotions to master, any passionate feeling to restrain.

All he now did was to take a shagreen case out of his breast pocket and hold it out towards her.

"Claire," he said quietly, "I have brought you, in memory of our wedding day, a little gift which I hope you will like. It is a medallion of the children." And as she at last advanced towards him, he pressed a spring, and revealed a dull gold medal on which, modelled in high relief, and superposed the one on the other, were Clairette's and Jacqueline's childish, delicately pure profiles.

A softer, kindlier light came into Claire de Wissant's sad grey eyes. She held out a hesitating hand—and Jacques de Wissant, before placing his gift in it, took that soft hand in his, and, bending rather awkwardly, kissed it lightly. In France, even now, a man will often kiss a woman's hand by way of conventional, respectful homage. But to Claire the touch of her husband's lips was hateful—so hateful indeed that she had to make an instant effort to hide the feeling of physical repulsion with which that touch had suddenly engulfed her in certain dark recesses of memory and revolt.

"It is a charming medallion," she said hurriedly, "quite a work of art, Jacques; and I thank you for having thought of it. It gives me great—very great pleasure."

And then something happened which was to her so utterly unexpected that she gave a stifled cry of pain—almost it seemed of fear.

As she forced herself to look straight into her husband's face, the anguish in her own sore heart unlocked the key to his, and she perceived with the eyes of the soul, which see, when they are not holden, so much that is concealed from the eyes of the body, the suffering, the dumb longing she had never allowed herself to know were there.

For the first time since her marriage—since that wedding day of which this was the tenth anniversary—Claire felt pity for Jacques as well as for herself. For the first time her rebellious heart acknowledged that her husband also was enmeshed in a web of tragic circumstance.

"Jacques?" she cried. "Oh, Jacques!" And as she so uttered his name twice, there came a look of acute distress and then of sudden resolution on her face. "I wish you to know," she exclaimed, "that—that—if I were a wicked woman I should perhaps be to you a better wife!" Thanks to the language in which she spoke, there was a play on the word—that word which in French signifies woman as well as wife.

He stared at her, and uttered no word of answer, of understanding, in response to her strange speech.

At one time, not lately, but many years ago, Claire had sometimes tried his patience by the odd, unreasonable things she said, and once, stung beyond bearing, he had told her so. Remembering those cold, measured words of rebuke, she now caught with quick, exultant relief at the idea that Jacques had not understood the half-confession wrung from her by her sudden vision of his pain; and she swung back to a belief she had always held till just now, the belief that he was dull—dull and unperceptive.

With a nervous smile she turned again to her mirror, and then Jacques de Wissant, with his wife's enigmatic words ringing in his ears, abruptly left the room.

As if pursued by some baneful presence, he hastened through Claire's beautiful boudoir, across the dining-room hung with the Gobelins tapestries which his wife had brought him as part of her slender dower, and so into the oval hall which formed the centre of the house.

And there Jacques de Wissant waited for a while, trying to still and to co-ordinate his troubled thoughts and impressions.

Ah yes, he had understood—understood only too well Claire's strange, ambiguous utterance! There are subtle, unbreathed temptations which all men and all women, when tortured by jealousy, not only understand but divine before they are actually in being.

Jacques de Wissant now believed that he was justified of the suspicions of which he had been ashamed. His wife—moved by some obscure desire for self-revelation to which he had had no clue—had flung at him the truth.

Yes, without doubt Claire could have made him happy—so little would have contented his hunger for her—had she been one of those light women of whom he sometimes heard, who go from their husbands' kisses to those of their lovers.

But if he sometimes, nay, often heard of them, Jacques de Wissant knew nothing of such women. The men of his race had known how to acquire honest wives, aye, and keep them so. There had never been in the de Wissant family any of those ugly scandals which stain other clans, and which are remembered over generations in French provincial towns. Those scandals which, if they provoke a laugh and cruel sneer when discussed by the indifferent, are recalled with long faces and anxious whisperings when a young girl's future is being discussed, and which make the honourable marriage of daughters difficult of achievement.

Jacques de Wissant thanked the God of his fathers that Claire had nothing in common with such women as those: he thought he did not need her assurance to know that his honour, in the usual, narrow sense of the phrase, was safe in her hands, but still her strange, imprudent words of half-avowal racked him with jealous and, yes, suspicious pain.

Fortunately for him, he was a man burdened with much business, and so at last he looked at his watch. Why, it was getting late—terribly late, and he prided himself on his punctuality. Still, if he started now, at once, he would be at the Hôtel de Ville a few minutes before ten o'clock, the time when the first of the civil marriages he had to celebrate that morning was timed to take place.

Without passing through the house, he made his way rapidly round by the gardens to the road, winding ribbon-wise behind the cliffs, where his phaeton was waiting for him; for Jacques de Wissant had as yet resisted the wish of his wife and the advice of those of his friends who considered that he ought to purchase an automobile: driving had been from boyhood one of his few pleasures and accomplishments.

But as he drove, keeping his fine black bays well in hand, the five miles into the town, and tried to fix his mind on a commercial problem of great importance with which he would be expected to deal that day, Jacques de Wissant found it impossible to think of any matter but that which for the moment filled his heart to the exclusion of all else. That matter concerned his own relations to his wife, and his wife's relations to Commander Dupré.

This gentleman of France was typical in more than one sense of his nation and of his class—quite unlike, that is, to the fancy picture which foreigners draw of the average Frenchman. Reserved and cold in manner; proud, with an intense but never openly expressed pride in his name and of what the bearers of it had achieved for their country; obstinate and narrow as are apt to be all human beings whose judgment is never questioned by those about them, Jacques de Wissant's fetish was his personal honour and the honour of his name —of the name of Wissant.

In his distress and disturbance of mind—for his wife's half confession had outraged his sense of what was decorous and fitting—his memory travelled over the map of his past life, aye, and even beyond the boundaries of his own life.

Before him lay spread retrospectively the story of his parents' uneventful, happy marriage. They had been mated in the good old French way, that is, up to their wedding morning they had never met save in the presence of their respective parents. And yet—and yet how devoted they had been to each other! So completely one in thought, in interest, in sympathy had they grown that when, after thirty-three years of married life, his father had died, Jacques' mother had not known how to go on living. She had slipped out of life a few months later, and as she lay dying she had used a very curious expression: "My faithful companion is calling me," she had said to her only child, "and you must not try, dear son, to make me linger on the way."

Now, to-day, Jacques de Wissant asked himself with perplexed pain and anger, why it was that his parents had led so peaceful, so dignified, so wholly contented a married life, while he himself——?

And yet his own marriage had been a love match—or so those about him had all said with nods and smiles—love marriages having suddenly become the fashion in the rich provincial world of which he had then been one of the heirs-apparent.

His old-fashioned mother would have preferred as daughter-in-law any one of half a dozen girls who belonged to her own good town of Falaise, and whom she had known from childhood. But Jacques had been difficult to please, and he was already thirty-two when he had met, by a mere chance, Claire de Kergouët at her first ball. She was only seventeen, with but the promise of a beauty which was now in exquisite flower, and he had decided, there and then, in the course of two hours, that this demoiselle de Kergouët was alone worthy of becoming Madame Jacques de Wissant.

And on the whole his prudent parents had blessed his choice, for the girl was of the best Breton stock, and came of a family famed in the naval annals of France. Unluckily Claire de Kergouët had had no dowry to speak of, for her father, the Admiral, had been a spendthrift, and, as is still the reckless Breton fashion, father of a large family—three daughters and four sons. But Jacques de Wissant had not allowed his parents to give the matter of

Claire's fortune more than a regretful thought—indeed, he had done further, he had "recognized" a larger dowry than she brought him to save the pride of her family.

But Claire—he could not help thinking of it to-day with a sense of bitter injury—had never seemed grateful, had never seemed to understand all that had been done for her. . . .

Had he not poured splendid gifts upon her in the beginning of their married life? And, what had been far more difficult, had he not, within reason, contented all her strange whims and fantasies?

But nought had availed him to secure even a semblance of that steadfast, warm affection, that sincere interest and pride in his concerns which is all such a Frenchman as was Jacques de Wissant expects, or indeed desires, of his wedded wife. Had Claire been such a woman, Jacques' own passion for her would soon have dulled into a reasonable, comfortable affection. But his wife's cool aloofness had kept alive the hidden fires, the more —so ironic are the tricks which sly Dame Nature plays—that for many years past he had troubled her but very little with his company.

Outwardly Claire de Wissant did her duty, entertaining his friends and relations on such occasions as was incumbent on her, and showing herself a devoted and careful mother to the twin daughters who formed the only vital link between her husband and herself. But inwardly? Inwardly they two were strangers.

And yet only during the last few months had Jacques de Wissant ever felt jealous of his wife. There had been times when he had been angered by the way in which her young beauty, her indefinable, mysterious charm, had attracted the very few men with whom she was brought into contact. But Claire, so her husband had always acknowledged to himself, was no flirt; she was ever perfectly "correct."

Correct was a word dear to Jacques de Wissant. It was one which he used as a synonym for great things — things such as honour, fineness of conduct, loyalty.

But fate had suddenly introduced a stranger into the dull, decorous life of the Pavillon de Wissant, and it was he, Jacques himself, who had brought him there.

How bitter it was to look back and remember how much he had liked—liked because he had respected—Commander Dupré! He now hated and feared the naval officer, and he would have given much to have been able to despise him. But that Jacques de Wissant could not do. Commander Dupré was still all that he had taken him to be when he first made him free of his house—a brilliant officer, devoted to his profession, already noted in the Service as having made several important inprovements in submarine craft.

From the first it had seemed peculiar, to Jacques de Wissant's mind unnatural, that such a man as was Dupré should be so keenly interested in music and in modern literature. But so it was, and it had been owing to these strange, untoward tastes that Commander Dupré and Claire had become friends.

He now reminded himself, for the hundredth time, that he had begun by actually approving of the acquaintance between his wife and the naval officer—an acquaintance which he had naturally supposed would be of the most "correct" nature.

Then, without warning, there came an hour —nay, a moment, when in that twilight hour which the French call "'Twixt dog and wolf," the most torturing and shameful of human passions, jealousy, had taken possession of Jacques de Wissant, disintegrating, rather than shattering, the elaborate fabric of his House of Life, that house in which he had always dwelt so snugly and unquestioningly ensconced.

He had come home after a long afternoon

spent at the Hôtel de Ville to learn with tepid pleasure that there was a visitor, Commander Dupré, in the house, and as he had come hurrying towards his wife's boudoir, Jacques had heard Claire's low, deep voice and the other's ardent, eager tones mingling together. . . .

And then as he, the husband, had opened the door, they had stopped speaking, their words clipped as if a sword had fallen between them. At the same moment a servant had brought a lamp into the twilit room, and Jacques had seen the ravaged face of Commander Dupré, a fair, tanned face full of revolt and of longing leashed. Claire had remained in shadow, but her eyes, or so the interloper thought he perceived, were full of tears.

Since that spring evening the Mayor of Falaise had not had an easy moment. While scorning to act the spy upon his wife, he was for ever watching her, and keeping an eager and yet scarcely conscious count of her movements.

True, Commander Dupré had soon ceased to trouble the owner of the Pavillon de Wissant by his presence. The younger officers came and went, but since that hour, laden with unspoken drama, their commander only came when good breeding required him to pay a formal call on his nearest neighbour and sometime host. But Claire saw Dupré constantly at the Châlet des Dunes, her sister's house, and she was both too proud and too indifferent, it appeared, to her husband's view of what a young married woman's conduct should be, to conceal the fact.

This openness on his wife's part was at once Jacques' consolation and opportunity for endless self-torture.

For three long miserable months he had wrestled with those ignoble questionings only the jealous know, now accepting as probable, now rejecting with angry self-rebuke, the thought that his wife suffered, perhaps even returned, Dupré's love. And to-day, instead of finding his jealousy allayed by her half-confidence, he felt more wretched than he had ever been.

His horses responded to his mood, and going down the steep hill which leads into the town of Falaise they shied violently at a heap of stones they had passed sedately a dozen times or more. Jacques de Wissant struck them several cruel blows with the whip he scarcely ever used, and the groom, looking furtively at his master's set face and blazing eyes, felt suddenly afraid.

III

It was one o'clock, and the last of the wedding parties had swept gaily out of the great *salle* of the Falaise town hall and so to the Cathedral across the market place.

Jacques de Wissant, with a feeling of relief, took off his tricolor badge of office. With the instinctive love of order which was characteristic of the man, he gathered up the papers that were spread on the large table and placed them in neat piles before him. Through the high windows, which by his orders had been prised open, for it was intensely hot, he could hear what seemed an unwonted stir outside. The picturesque town was full of strangers; in addition to the usual holiday-makers from the neighbourhood, crowds of Parisians had come down to spend the Feast of the Assumption by the sea.

The Mayor of Falaise liked to hear this unwonted stir and movement, for everything that affected the prosperity of the town affected him very nearly; but he was constitutionally averse to noise, and just now he felt very tired. The varied emotions which had racked him that morning had drained him of his vitality; and he thought with relief that in a few moments he would be in the old-fashioned restaurant just across the market place, where a table was always reserved for him when his town house happened to be shut up, and where all his tastes and dietetic fads—for M. de Wissant had a delicate digestion—were known.

He took up his tall hat and his lemon-coloured gloves—and then a look of annoyance came over his weary face, for he heard the swinging of a door. Evidently his clerk was coming back to ask some stupid question.

He always found it difficult to leave the town hall at the exact moment he wished to do so; for although the officials dreaded his cold reprimands, they were far more afraid of his sudden hot anger if business of any importance were done without his knowledge and sanction.

But this time it was not his clerk who wished to intercept the mayor on his way out to *déjeuner;* it was the chief of the employés in the telephone and telegraph department of the building, a forward, pushing young man whom Jacques de Wissant disliked.

"M'sieur le maire?" and then he stopped short, daunted by the mayor's stern look of impatient fatigue. "Has m'sieur le maire heard the news?" The speaker gathered up courage ; it is exciting to be the bearer of news, especially of ill news.

M. de Wissant shook his head.

"Alas! there has been an accident, m'sieur le maire! A terrible accident! One of the submarines—they don't yet know which it is—has been struck by a big private yacht and has sunk in the fairway of the Channel, about two miles out!"

The Mayor of Falaise uttered an involuntary exclamation of horror. "When did it happen?" he asked quickly.

"About half an hour ago more or less. *I* said that m'sieur le maire ought to be informed at once of such a calamity. But I was told to wait till the marriages were over."

Looking furtively at the mayor's pale face, the young man regretted that he had not taken more on himself, for m'sieur le maire looked seriously displeased.

There was an old feud between the municipal and the naval authorities of Falaise—there often is in a naval port—and the mayor ought certainly to have been among the very first to hear the news of the disaster.

The bearer of ill news hoped m'sieur le maire would not blame him for the delay, or cause the fact to postpone his advancement to a higher grade—that advancement which is the perpetual dream of every French Government official.

"The admiral has only just driven by," he observed insinuatingly, "not five minutes ago——"

But still Jacques de Wissant did not move. He was listening to the increasing stir and tumult going on outside in the market place. The sounds had acquired a sinister significance; he knew now that the tramping of feet, the loud murmur of voices, meant that the whole population belonging to the seafaring portion of the town was emptying itself out and hurrying towards the harbour and the shore.

Shaking off the bearer of ill news with a curt word of thanks, the Mayor of Falaise strode out of the town hall into the street and joined the eager crowd, mostly consisting of fisher folk, which grew denser as it swept down the tortuous narrow streets leading to the sea.

The people parted with a sort of rough respect to make way for their mayor; many of them, nay the majority, were known by name to Jacques de Wissant, and the older men and women among them could remember him as a child.

Rising to the tragic occasion, he walked forward with his head held high, and a look of deep concern on his pale, set face. The men who manned the Northern Submarine Flotilla were almost all men born and bred at Falaise—Falaise famed for the gallant sailors she has ever given to France.

The hurrying crowd—strangely silent in its haste—poured out on to the great stone-paved quays in which is set the harbour so finely encircled on two sides by the cliffs which give the town its name.

Beyond the harbour—crowded with shipping, and now alive with eager little craft and fishing-boats making ready to start for the scene of the calamity—lay a vast expanse of glistening sea, and on that sun-flecked blue pall every eye was fixed.

The end of the harbour jetty was already roped off, only those officially privileged being allowed through to the platform where now stood Admiral de Saint Vilquier impatiently waiting for the tug which was to take him out to the spot where the disaster had taken place. The Admiral was a naval officer of the old school—of the school who called their men "my children"—and who detested the Republican form of government as being subversive of discipline.

As Jacques de Wissant hurried up to him, he turned and stiffly saluted the Mayor of Falaise.

Admiral de Saint Vilquier had no liking for M. de Wissant—a cold prig of a fellow, and yet married to such a beautiful, such a charming young woman, the daughter, too, of one of the Admiral's oldest friends, of that Admiral de Kergouët with whom he had first gone to sea a matter of fifty years ago! The lovely Claire de Kergouët had been worthy of a better fate than to be wife to this plain, cold-blooded landsman.

"Do they yet know, Admiral, which of the submarines has gone down?" asked Jacques de Wissant in a low tone. He was full of a burning curiosity edged with a longing and a suspense into whose secret sources he had no wish to thrust a probe.

The Admiral's weather-beaten face was a shade less red than usual; the bright blue eyes he turned on the younger man were veiled with a film of moisture. "Yes, the news has just come in, but it isn't to be made public for awhile. It's the submarine *Neptune* which was struck, with Commander Dupré, Lieutenant Paritot, and ten men on board. The craft is lying eighteen fathoms deep——"

Jacques de Wissant uttered an inarticulate cry—was it of horror or only of surprise? And yet, gifted for that once and that once only with a kind of second sight, he had known that it was the *Neptune* and Commander Dupré which lay eighteen fathoms deep on the floor of the sea.

The old seaman, moved by the mayor's emotion, relaxed into a confidential undertone. "Poor Dupré! I had forgotten that you knew him. He is indeed pursued by a malignant fate. As of course you are aware, he applied a short time ago to be transferred to Toulon, and his appointment is in to-day's *Gazette*. In fact he was actually leaving Falaise this very evening in order to spend a week with his family before taking up his new command!"

The Mayor of Falaise stared at the Admiral. "Dupré going away?—leaving Falaise?" he repeated incredulously.

The other nodded.

Jacques de Wissant drew a long, deep breath. God! How mistaken he had been! Mistaken as no man, no husband, had ever been mistaken before. He felt overwhelmed, shaken with conflicting emotions in which shame and intense relief predominated.

The fact that Commander Dupré had applied for promotion was to his mind absolute proof that there had been nothing—nothing and less than nothing—between the naval officer and Claire. The Admiral's words now made it clear that he, Jacques de Wissant, had built up a huge superstructure of jealousy and base thoughts on the fact that poor Dupré and Claire had innocently enjoyed certain tastes in common. True, such friendships—friendships between unmarried men and attractive young married women—are generally speaking to be deprecated. Still, Claire had always been "correct;" of that there could now be no doubt.

As he stood there on the pier, staring out, as all those about him and behind him were doing, at the expanse of dark blue sun-flecked sea, there came over Jacques de Wissant a great lightening of the spirit. . . .

But all too soon his mind, his memory, swung back to the tragic business of the moment.

Suddenly the Admiral burst into speech, addressing himself, rather than the silent man by his side.

"The devil of it is," he exclaimed, "that the nearest salvage appliances are at Cherbourg! Thank God, the Ministry of Marine are alone responsible for that blunder. Dupré and his comrades have, it seems, thirty-six hours' supply of oxygen—if, indeed, they are still living, which I feel tempted to hope they are not. You see, Monsieur de Wissant, I was at Bizerta when the *Lutin* sank. A man doesn't want to remember two such incidents in his career. One is quite bad enough!"

"I suppose it isn't yet known how far the *Neptune* is injured?" inquired the Mayor of Falaise.

But he spoke mechanically; he was not really thinking of what he was saying. His inner and real self were still steeped in that strange mingled feeling of shame and relief—shame that he should have suspected his wife, exultant relief that his jealousy should have been so entirely unfounded.

"No, as usual no one knows exactly what did happen. But we shall learn something of that presently. The divers are on their way. But—but even if the craft did sustain no injury, what can they do? Ants might as well attempt to pierce a cannon-ball"—he shrugged his shoulders, oppressed by the vision his homely simile had conjured up.

And then—for no particular reason, save that his wife Claire was very present to him—Jacques de Wissant bethought himself that it was most unlikely that any tidings of the accident could yet have reached the Châlet des Dunes, the lonely villa on the shore where Claire was now lunching with her sister. But at any moment some casual visitor from the town might come out there with the sad news. He told himself uneasily that it would be well, if possible, to save his wife from such a shock. After all, Claire and that excellent Commander Dupré had been good friends—so much must be admitted, nay, now he was eager to admit it.

Jacques de Wissant touched the older man on the arm.

"I should be most grateful, Admiral, for the loan of your motor-car. I have just remembered that I ought to go home for an hour. This terrible affair made me forget it; but I shall not be long—indeed, I must soon be back, for there will be all sorts of arrangements to be made at the town hall. Of course we shall be besieged with inquiries, with messages from Paris, with telegrams——"

"My car, monsieur, is entirely at your disposal."

The Admiral could not help feeling, even at so sad and solemn a moment as this, a little satirical amusement. Arrangements at the town hall, forsooth! If the end of the world were in sight, the claims of the municipality of Falaise would not be neglected or forgotten; in as far as Jacques de Wissant could arrange it, everything in such a case would be ready at the town hall, if not on the quarter-deck, for the Great Assize!

What had a naval disaster to do with the

Mayor of Falaise, after all? But in this matter the old Admiral allowed prejudice to get the better of him; the men now immured in the submarine were, with two exceptions—their commander and his junior officer—all citizens of the town. It was their mothers, wives, children, sweethearts, who were now pressing with wild, agonized faces against the barriers drawn across the end of the pier. . . .

As Jacques de Wissant made his way through the crowd, his grey frock-coat was pulled by many a horny hand, and imploring faces gazed with piteous questioning into his. But he could give them no comfort.

Not till he found himself actually in the Admiral's car did he give his instructions to the chauffeur.

"Take me to the Châlet des Dunes as quickly as you can drive without danger," he said briefly. "You probably know where it is?"

The man nodded and looked round consideringly. He had never driven so elegantly attired a gentleman before. Why, M. de Wissant looked like a bridegroom! The Mayor of Falaise should be good for a handsome tip.

The chauffeur did not need to be told that on such a day time was of importance, and once they were out of the narrow, tortuous streets of the town, the Admiral's car flew.

And then, for the first time that day, Jacques de Wissant began to feel pleasantly cool, nay, there even came over him a certain exhilaration. He had been foolish to hold out against motor-cars. There was a great deal to be said for them, after all. He owed his wife reparation for his evil thoughts of her. He resolved that he would get Claire the best automobile money could buy. It is always a mistake to economize in such matters. . . .

His mind took a sudden turn—he felt ashamed of his egoism, and the sensation disturbed him, for the Mayor of Falaise very seldom had occasion to feel ashamed, either of his thoughts or of his actions. How could he have allowed his attention to stray from the subject which should just now be absorbing his whole mind?

Thirty-six hours' supply of oxygen? Well, it might have been worse, for a great deal can be done in thirty-six hours.

True, all the salvage appliances, so the Admiral had said, were at Cherbourg. What a shameful lack of forethought on someone's part! Still, there was little doubt but that the *Neptune* would be raised in—in time. The British Navy would send her salvage appliances.

Jacques de Wissant had a traditional distrust of the English, but at such moments all men are brothers, and just now the French and the English happened to be allies. He himself felt far more kindly to his little girls' governess, Miss Doughty, than he would have done five years ago.

Yes, without doubt the gallant English Navy would send salvage appliances. . . .

There would be some hours of suspense—terrible hours for the wives and mothers of the men, but those poor women would be upheld by the universal sympathy shown them. He himself as mayor of the town would do all he could. He would seek these poor women out, say consoling, hopeful things, and Claire would help him. She had, as he knew, a very tender heart, especially where seamen were concerned.

Indeed, it was a terrible thought—that of those brave fellows down there beneath the surface of the waters. Terrible, that is, if they were alive—alive in the same measure as he, Jacques de Wissant, was now alive in the keen, rushing air. Alive, and waiting for a deliverance that might never come. The idea made him feel a queer, interior tremor.

Then his mind, in spite of himself, swung back to its old moorings. How strange that he had not been told that Commander Dupré had applied for a change of command! Doubtless the Mediterranean was better suited, being a tideless sea, for submarine experiments. Keen, clever Dupré, absorbed as he was in his profession, had doubtless thought of that.

But, again, how odd of Claire not to have mentioned that Dupré was leaving Falaise! Of course it was possible that she also had been ignorant of the fact. She very seldom spoke of other people's affairs, and lately she had been so dreadfully worried about her sister's, Marie-Anne's, illness.

If his wife had known nothing of Commander Dupré's plans, it proved as hardly anything else could have done how little real intimacy there could have been between them. A man never leaves the woman he loves unless he has grown tired of her—then, as all the world knows, except perchance the poor soul herself, no place is too far for him to make for.

Such was Jacques de Wissant's simple, cynical philosophy concerning a subject to which he had never given much thought. The tender passion had always appeared to him in one of two shapes—the one was a grotesque and slightly improper shape, which makes men do silly, absurd things; the other came in the semblance of a sinister demon which wrecks the honour and devastates, as nothing else can do, the happiness of respectable families. It was this second and more hateful form which had haunted him these last few weeks.

He recalled with a sick feeling of distaste the state of mind and body he had been in that very morning. Why, he had then been in the mood to kill Dupré, or, at any rate, to welcome the news of his death with fierce joy! And then, simultaneously with his discovery of how groundless had been his jealousy, he had learnt the awful fact that the man whom he had wrongly accused lay out there, buried and yet alive, beneath the glistening sea, which was stretched out, like a great blue pall, on his left.

Still, it was only proper that his wife should be spared the shock of hearing in some casual way of this awful accident. Claire had always been sensitive, curiously so, to everything that concerned the Navy. Admiral de Saint Vilquier had recalled the horrible submarine disaster of Bizerta harbour; Jacques de Wissant now remembered uncomfortably how very unhappy that sad affair had made Claire. Why, one day he had found her in a passion of tears, mourning over the tragic fate of those poor sailor men, the crew of the *Lutin*, of whose very names she was ignorant!

At the time he had thought her betrayal of feeling very unreasonable, but now he understood, and even shared to a certain extent, the pain she had shown; but then he knew Dupré, knew and liked him, and the men immured in the *Neptune* were men of Falaise.

These were the thoughts which jostled each other in Jacques de Wissant's brain as he sat back in the Admiral's car.

They were now rushing past the Pavillon de Wissant. What a pity it was that Claire had not remained quietly at home to-day! It would have been so much pleasanter—if one could think of anything being pleasant in such a connection—to have gone in and told her the sad news at home. Her sister, Madeleine Baudoin, though older than Claire, was foolishly emotional and unrestrained in the expression of her feelings. Madeleine was sure to make a scene when she heard of Commander Dupré's peril, and Jacques de Wissant hated scenes.

He now asked himself whether there was any real necessity for his telling his wife before her sister. All he need do was to send Claire a message by the servant who opened the door to him. He would say that she was wanted at home; she would think something had happened to one of the children, and this would be a good thing, for it would prepare her in a measure for ill tidings.

From what Jacques knew of his wife he believed she would receive the news quietly, and he, her husband, would show her every consideration; again he reminded himself that it would be ridiculous to deny the fact that Claire had made a friend, almost an intimate, of Commander Dupré. It would be natural, nay "correct," for her to be greatly distressed when she heard of the accident.

There came a familiar cutting in the road, and again the sea lay spread out, an opaque, glistening sheet of steel, before him. He gazed across, with a feeling of melancholy and fearful curiosity, to the swarm of craft great and small collected round the place where the *Neptune* lay, eighteen fathoms deep. . . .

He hoped Claire would not ask to go back into the town with him in order to hear the latest news. But if she did so ask, then he would raise no objection. Every Falaise woman, whatever her rank in life, was now full of suspense and anxiety, and as the mayor's wife Claire had a right to share that anxious suspense.

The car was now slowing on the sharp decline leading to the shore, and Jacques de

Wissant got up and touched the chauffeur on the shoulder.

"Stop here," he said. "You needn't drive down to the Châlet. I want you to turn and wait for me at the Pavillon de Wissant. Ask my servants to give you some luncheon. I may be half an hour or more, but I want to get back to Falaise as soon as I can."

The Châlet des Dunes had been well named. It stood enclosed in rough palings in a sandy wilderness. An attempt had been made to turn the immediate surroundings of the villa into the semblance of a garden; there were wind-blown flowers set in sandy flower-beds, and coarse, luxuriant creepers flung their long, green ropes about the wooden verandah. In front, stretching out into the sea, was a stone pier, built by Jacques' father many a year ago.

The Châlet looked singularly quiet and deserted, for all the shutters had been closed in order to shut out the midday heat.

Jacques de Wissant became vaguely uneasy. He reconsidered his plan of action. If the two sisters were alone together—as he supposed them to be—he would go in and quietly tell them of the accident. It would be making altogether too much of the matter to send for Claire to come out to him; she might very properly resent it. For the matter of that, it was quite possible that Madeleine Baudoin had some little sentiment for Dupré. That would explain so much—the officer's constant presence at the Châlet des Dunes added to his absence from the Pavillon. It was odd he had never thought of the possibility before.

But this new idea made Jacques grow more and more uneasy at the thought of the task which now lay before him. With slow, hesitating steps he walked up to the little front door of the Châlet.

He pulled the rusty bell-handle. How absurd to have ironwork in such a place!

There followed what seemed to him a very long pause. He rang again.

There came the sound of light, swift steps; he could hear them in spite of the rhythmical surge of the sea; and then the door was opened by his sister-in-law, Madame Baudoin, herself.

In the midst of his own agitation and unease, Jacques de Wissant saw that there was a look of embarrassment on the face which Madeleine tried to make amiably welcoming.

"Jacques?" she exclaimed. "Forgive me for having made you ring twice! I have sent the servants into Falaise to purchase a railway time-table. Claire will doubtless have told you that I am starting for Italy to-night. Our poor

Marie-Anne is worse; and I feel that it is my duty to go to her."

She did not step aside to allow him to come in. In fact, doubtless without meaning to do so, she was actually blocking up the door.

No, Claire had not told Jacques that Marie-Anne was worse. That of course was why she had looked so unhappy this morning. He felt hurt and angered by his wife's reserve.

"I am sure you will agree, Madeleine," he said stiffly—he was not sorry to gain a little time—"that it would not be wise for Claire to accompany you to Italy. After all, she is still quite a young woman, and poor Marie-Anne's disease is most infectious. I have ascertained, too, that there is a regular epidemic raging in Mantua."

Madeleine nodded. Then she turned, with an uneasy side-look at her brother-in-law, and began leading the way down the short passage. The door of the dining-room was open; Jacques could not help seeing that only one place was laid at the round table, also that Madeleine had just finished her luncheon.

"Isn't Claire here?" he asked, surprised. "She said she was going to lunch with you to-day. Hasn't she been here this morning?"

"No—I mean yes." Madeleine spoke confusedly. "She did not stay to lunch. She was only here for a very little while."

"But has she gone home again?"

"Well—she may be home by now; I really don't know"—Madeleine was opening the door of the little drawing-room.

It was an ugly, common-looking room; the walls were hung with Turkey red, and ornamented with cheap coloured prints. There were cane and basket chairs which Madame Baudoin had striven to make comfortable with the help of cushions and rugs.

Jacques de Wissant told himself that it was odd that Claire should like to spend so much of her time here, in the Châlet des Dunes, instead of asking her sister to join her each morning or afternoon in her own beautiful house on the cliff.

"Forgive me," he said stiffly, "but I can't stay a moment. I really came for Claire. You say I shall find her at home?"

He held his top hat and his yellow gloves in his hand, and his sister-in-law thought she had never seen Jacques look so plain and unattractive, and—and tiresome as he looked to-day.

Madame Baudoin had a special reason for wishing him away; but she knew the slow, sure workings of his mind. If Jacques found that his wife had not gone back to the Pavillon de Wissant, and that there was no news of her there, he would almost certainly come back to the Châlet des Dunes for further information.

"No," she said reluctantly, "Claire has not gone back to the Pavillon. I believe that she has gone into the town. She had something important that she wished to do there."

She looked so troubled, so—so uncomfortable that Jacques de Wissant leapt to the sudden conclusion that the tidings he had been at such pains to bring had already been brought to the Châlet des Dunes.

"Ah!" he exclaimed, "then I am too late! Ill news travels fast."

"Ill news?" Madeleine repeated affrightedly. "Is anything the matter? Has anything happened to one of the children? Don't keep me in suspense, Jacques. I am not cold-blooded—like you!"

"The children are all right," he said shortly. "But there has been, as you evidently know, an accident. The submarine *Neptune* has met with a serious mishap. She now lies with her crew in eighteen fathoms of water about two miles out."

He spoke with cold acerbity. How childishly foolish of Madeleine to try and deceive him! But all women of the type to which she belonged make foolish mysteries about nothing.

"The submarine *Neptune?*" As she stammered out the question which had already been answered, there came over Madame Baudoin's face a look of measureless terror. Twice her lips opened—and twice she closed them again.

At last she uttered a few words—words of anguished protest and revolt. "No, no," she cried, "that can't be—it's impossible!"

"Command yourself!" he said sternly. "Remember what would be thought by anyone who saw you in this state."

But she went on looking at him with wild, terror-stricken eyes. "My poor Claire!" she moaned. "My little sister Claire——"

All Jacques de Wissant's jealousy leapt into eager, quivering life. Then he had been right after all? His wife loved Dupré. Her sister's anguished sympathy had betrayed Claire's secret as nothing Claire herself was ever likely to say or do could have done.

"You are a good sister," he said ironically, "to take Claire's distress so much to heart. Identifying yourself as entirely as you seem to do with her, I am surprised that you did not accompany her into Falaise: it was most wrong of you to let her go alone."

"Claire is not in Falaise," muttered Madeleine. She was grasping the back of one of the cane chairs with her hand as if glad of even that slight support, staring at him with a dazed look of abject misery which increased his anger, his disgust.

"Not in Falaise?" he echoed sharply. "Then where, in God's name, is she?"

A most disagreeable possibility had flashed into his mind. Was it conceivable that his wife had had herself rowed to the scene of the disaster? If she had done that, if her sister had allowed her to go alone, or accompanied maybe by one or other of the officers belonging to the submarine flotilla, then he told himself with jealous rage that he would find it very difficult ever to forgive Claire. There are things a woman with any self-respect, especially a woman who is the mother of daughters, refrains from doing.

"Well?" he said contemptuously. "Well, Madeleine? I am waiting to hear the truth. I desire no explanations—no excuses. I cannot, however, withhold myself from telling you that you ought to have accompanied your sister, even if you found it impossible to control her."

"I was there yesterday," said Madeleine Baudoin, with a pinched, white face, "for over two hours."

"What do you mean?" he asked suspiciously. "Where were you yesterday for over two hours?"

"In the *Neptune*."

She gazed at him, past him, with widely open eyes, as if she were staring, fascinated, at some scene of unutterable horror—and there crept into Jacques de Wissant's mind a thought so full of shameful dread that he thrust it violently from him.

"You were in the *Neptune*," he said slowly, "knowing well that it is absolutely forbidden for any officer to take a friend on board a submarine without a special permit from the Minister of Marine?"

"It is sometimes done," she said listlessly.

Madame Baudoin had now sat down on a low chair, and she was plucking at the front of her white serge skirt with a curious mechanical movement of the fingers.

"Did the submarine actually put out to sea with you on board?"

She nodded her head, and then very deliberately added, "Yes, I have told you that I was out for two hours. They all knew it—the men and officers of the flotilla. I was horribly frightened, but—but now I am glad indeed that I went. Yes, I am indeed glad!"

"Why are you glad?" he asked roughly—and again a hateful suspicion thrust itself insistently upon him.

"I am glad I went, because it will make

what Claire has done to-day seem natural, a —a simple escapade."

There was a moment of terrible silence between them.

"Then do all the officers and men belonging to the flotilla know that my wife is out there—in the *Neptune?*" Jacques de Wissant asked in a low, still voice.

"No," said Madeleine, and there was now a look of shame, as well as of terror, on her face. "They none of them know—only those who are on board." She hesitated a moment—"That is why I sent the servants away this morning. We—I mean Commander Dupré and I—did not think it necessary that anyone should know."

"Then no one—that is, only a hare-brained young officer and ten men belonging to the town of Falaise—were to be aware of the fact that my wife had accompanied her lover on this life-risking expedition? You and Dupré were indeed tender of her honour—and mine."

"Jacques!" She took her hand off the chair, and faced her brother-in-law proudly. "What infamous thing is this that you are harbouring in your mind? My sister is an honest woman, aye, as honest, as high-minded as was your own mother——"

He stopped her with a violent gesture. "Do

not mention Claire and my mother in the same breath!" he cried.

"Ah, but I will—I must! You want the truth—you said just now you wanted only the truth. Then you shall hear the truth! Yes, it is as you have evidently suspected. Louis Dupré loves Claire, and she"—her voice faltered, then grew firmer—"she may have had for him a little sentiment. Who can tell? You have not been at much pains to make her happy. But what is true, what is certain, is that she rejected his love. To-day they were to part—for ever."

Her voice failed again, then once more it strengthened and hardened.

"That is why he in a moment of folly—I admit it was in a moment of folly—asked her to come out on his last cruise in the *Neptune*. When you came I was expecting them back any moment. But, Jacques, do not be afraid. I swear to you that no one shall ever know. Admiral de Saint Vilquier will do anything for us Kergouëts; I myself will go to him, and—and explain."

But Jacques de Wissant scarcely heard the eager, pitiful words.

He had thrust his wife from his mind, and her place had been taken by his honour—his honour and that of his children, of happy, light-hearted Clairette and Jacqueline. For what seemed a long while he said nothing; then, with all the anger gone from his voice, he spoke, uttered a fiat.

"No," he said quietly. "You must leave the Admiral to me, Madeleine. You were going to Italy to-night, were you not? That, I take it, *is* true."

She nodded impatiently. What did her proposed journey to Italy matter compared with her beloved Claire's present peril?

"Well, you must carry out your plan, my poor Madeleine. You must go away to-night."

She stared at him, her face at last blotched with tears, and a look of bewildered anguish in her eyes.

"You must do this," Jacques de Wissant went on deliberately, "for Claire's sake, and for the sake of Claire's children. You haven't sufficient self-control to endure suspense calmly, secretly. You need not go farther than Paris, but those whom it concerns will be told that Claire has gone with you to Italy. There will always be time to tell the truth. Meanwhile, the Admiral and I will devise a plan. And perhaps"—he waited a moment—"the truth will never be known, or only known to a very few people—people who, as you say, will understand."

He had spoken very slowly, as if weighing each of his words, but it was quickly, with a queer catch in his voice, that he added—"I ask you to do this, my sister"—he had never before called Madeleine Baudoin "my sister"—"because of Claire's children, of Clairette and Jacqueline. Their mother would not wish a slur to rest upon them."

She looked at him with piteous, hunted eyes. But she knew that she must do what he asked.

IV

Jacques de Wissant sat at his desk in the fine old room which is set aside for the mayor's sole use in the town hall of Falaise.

He was waiting for Admiral de Saint Vilquier, whom he had summoned on the plea of a matter both private and urgent. In his note, of which he had written more than one draft, he had omitted none of the punctilio usual in French official correspondence, and he had asked pardon, in the most formal language, for asking the Admiral to come to him, instead of proposing to go to the Admiral.

The time that had elapsed since he had parted from his sister-in-law had seemed like years instead of hours, and yet every moment of those hours had been filled with action.

From the Châlet des Dunes Jacques had made his way straight to the Pavillon de Wissant, and there his had been the bitter task of lying to his household.

They had accepted unquestioningly his statement that their mistress, without waiting even to go home, had left the Châlet des Dunes with her sister for Italy owing to the arrival of sudden worse news from Mantua.

While Claire's luggage was being by his orders hurriedly prepared, he had changed his clothes; and then, overcome with mortal weariness, with sick, sombre suspense, he had returned to Falaise, taking the railway station on his way to the town hall, and from there going through the grim comedy of despatching his wife's trunks to Paris.

Since the day war was declared by France on Germany, there had never been at the town hall of Falaise so busy an afternoon. Urgent messages of inquiry and condolence came pouring in from all over the civilized world, and the mayor had to compose suitable answers to them all.

To him there also fell the painful duty of officially announcing to the crowd surging impatiently in the market place—though room in front was always made and kept for those of the fisher folk who had relatives in the submarine service—that it was the *Neptune* which had gone down.

He had seen the effect of that announcement painted on rough, worn, upturned faces; he had heard the cries of anger, the groans of despair of the few, and had witnessed the relief, the tears of joy of the many. But his heart felt numb, and his cold, stern manner kept the emotions and excitement of those about him in check.

At last there had come a short respite. It was publicly announced that owing to the currents the divers had had to suspend their work awhile, but that salvage appliances from England and from Cherbourg were on their way to Falaise, and that it was hoped by seven that evening active operations would begin. With luck the *Neptune* might be raised before midnight.

Fortunate people blessed with optimistic natures were already planning a banquet at which the crew of the *Neptune* were to be entertained within an hour of the rescue.

Jacques de Wissant rose from the massive First Empire table which formed part of the fine suite of furniture presented by the great

Napoleon just a hundred years ago to the municipality of Falaise.

With bent head, his hands clasped behind him, the mayor began walking up and down the long room.

Admiral de Saint Vilquier might now come at any moment, but the man awaiting him had not yet made up his mind how to word what he had to say—how much to tell, how much to conceal from, his wife's old friend. He was only too well aware that if the desperate attempts which would soon be made to raise the *Neptune* were successful, and if its human freight were rescued alive, the fact that there had been a woman on board could not be concealed. Thousands would know to-night, and millions to-morrow morning.

Not only would the amazing story provide newspaper readers all over the world with a thrilling, unexpected piece of news, but the fact that there had been a woman involved in the disaster would be perpetuated, as long as our civilization endures, in every account of subsequent accidents to submarine craft.

More intimately, vividly agonizing was the knowledge that the story, the scandal, would be revived when there arose the all-important question of a suitable marriage for Clairette or Jacqueline.

As he paced up and down the room, longing for and yet dreading the coming of the Admiral, he visualized what would happen. He could almost hear the whispered words: "Yes, dear friend, the girl is admirably brought up, and has a large fortune, also she and your son have taken quite a fancy for one another, but there is that very ugly story of the mother! Don't you remember that she was with her lover in the submarine *Neptune*? The citizens of Falaise still laugh at the story and point her out in the street. Like mother like daughter, you know!" Thus the miserable man tortured himself, turning the knife in his wound.

But stay—— Supposing the salvage appliances failed, as they had failed at Bizerta, to raise the *Neptune*? Then with the help of Admiral de Saint Vilquier the awful truth might be kept secret.

At last the door opened.

Jacques de Wissant took a step forward, and as his hand rested loosely for a moment in the old seaman's firmer grasp, he would have given many years of his life to postpone the coming interview.

"As you asked me so urgently to do so, I have come, M. de Wissant, to learn what you have to tell me. But I'm afraid the time I can spare you must be short. As you know, I am to be at the station in half an hour to meet the Minister of Marine. He will probably wish to go out at once to the scene of the calamity, and I shall have to accompany him."

The Admiral was annoyed at having been thus sent for to the town hall. It was surely Jacques de Wissant's place to have come to him.

And then, while listening to the other's murmured excuses, the old naval officer happened to look straight into the face of the Mayor of Falaise, and at once a change came over his manner, even his voice softened and altered.

"Pardon my saying so, M. de Wissant," he exclaimed abruptly, "but you look extremely ill! You mustn't allow this sad business to take such a hold on you. It is tragic no doubt that such things must be, but remember"—he uttered the words solemnly—"they are the Price of Admiralty."

"I know, I know," muttered Jacques de Wissant.

"Shall we sit down?"

The deadly pallor, the look of strain on the face of the man before him was making the Admiral feel more and more uneasy. "It would be very awkward," he thought to himself, "were Jacques de Wissant to be taken ill, here, now, with me—— Ah, I have it!"

Then he said aloud, "You have doubtless had nothing to eat since the morning?" And as de Wissant nodded—"But that's absurd! It's always madness to go without food. Believe me, you will want all your strength during the next few days. As for me, I had fortunately lunched before I received the sad news. I keep to the old hours; I do not care for your English *déjeuners* at one o'clock. Midday is late enough for me!"

"Admiral?" said the wretched man, "Admiral——?"

"Yes, take your time; I am not really in such a hurry. I am quite at your disposal."

"It is a question of honour," muttered Jacques de Wissant, "a question of honour, Admiral, or I should not trouble you with the matter."

Admiral de Saint Vilquier leant forward, but Jacques de Wissant avoided meeting the shrewd, searching eyes.

"The honour of a naval family is involved." The Mayor of Falaise was now speaking in a low, pleading voice.

The Admiral stiffened. "Ah!" he exclaimed. "So you have been asked to intercede with me on behalf of some young scapegrace. Well, who is it? I'll look into the matter to-morrow morning. I really cannot think of anything to-day but of this terrible business——"

"—— Admiral, it concerns this business."

"The loss of the *Neptune?* In what way can the honour of a naval family be possibly involved in such a matter?" There was a touch of hauteur as well as of indignant surprise in the fine old seaman's voice.

"Admiral," said Jacques de Wissant deliberately, "there was—there is—a woman on board the *Neptune.*"

"A woman in the *Neptune?* That is quite impossible!" The Admiral got up from his chair. "It is one of our strictest regulations that no stranger be taken on board a submarine without a special permit from the Minister of Marine, countersigned by an admiral. No such permit has been issued for many months. In no case would a woman be allowed on board. Commander Dupré is far too conscientious, too loyal, an officer to break such a regulation."

"Commander Dupré," said Jacques de Wissant in a low, bitter tone, "was not too conscientious or too loyal an officer to break that regulation, for there is, I repeat it, a woman in the *Neptune.*"

The Admiral sat down again. "But this is serious—very serious," he muttered.

He was thinking of the effect, not only at home but abroad, of such a breach of discipline.

He shook his head with a pained, angry gesture—"I understand what happened," he said at last. "The woman was of course poor Dupré's"—and then something in Jacques de Wissant's pallid face made him substitute, for the plain word he meant to have used, a softer, kindlier phrase—"poor Dupré's *bonne amie*," he said.

"I am advised not," said Jacques de Wissant shortly. "I am told that the person in question is a young lady."

"Do you mean an unmarried girl?" asked the Admiral. There was great curiosity and sincere relief in his voice.

"I beg of you not to ask me, Admiral! The family of the lady have implored me to reveal as little of the truth as possible. They have taken their own measures, and they are good measures, to account for her—her disappearance." The unhappy man spoke with considerable agitation.

"Quite so! Quite so! They are right. I have no wish to show indiscreet curiosity."

"Do you think anything can be done to

prevent the fact becoming known?" asked Jacques de Wissant — and, as the other waited a moment before answering, the suspense became almost more than he could endure.

He got up and instinctively stood with his back to the light. "The family of this young lady are willing to make any pecuniary sacrifice——"

"It is not a question of pecuniary sacrifice," the Admiral said stiffly. "Money will never really purchase either secrecy or silence. But honour, M. de Wissant, will sometimes, nay, often, do both."

"Then you think the fact can be concealed?"

"I think it will be impossible to conceal it if the *Neptune* is raised"—he hesitated, and his voice sank as he added the poignant words "*in time*. But if that happens, though I fear that it is not likely to happen, then I promise you that I will allow it to be thought that I had given this lady permission, and her improper action will be accepted for what it no doubt was—a foolish escapade. If Dupré and little Paritot are the men of honour I take them to be, one or other of them will of course marry her!"

"And if the *Neptune* is not raised—" the

Mayor's voice also dropped to a whisper—"*in time*—what then?"

"Then," said the Admiral, "everything will be done by me—so you can assure your unlucky friends—to conceal the fact that Commander Dupré failed in his duty. Not for his sake, you understand—he, I fear, deserves what he has suffered, what he is perhaps still suffering,"—a look of horror stole over his old, weather-roughened face—"but for the sake of the foolish girl and for the sake of her family. You say it is a naval family?"

"Yes," said Jacques de Wissant. "A noted naval family."

The Admiral got up. "And now I, on my side, must exact of you a pledge, M. de Wissant—" he looked searchingly at the Government official standing before him. "I solemnly implore you, monsieur, to keep this fact you have told me absolutely secret for the time being—secret even from the Minister of Marine."

The Mayor of Falaise bent his head. "I intend to act," he said slowly, "as if I had never heard it."

"I ask it for the honour, the repute, of the Service," muttered the old officer. "After all, M. de Wissant, the poor fellow did not mean much harm. We sailors have all, at different times of our lives, had some *bonne amie* whom we found it devilish hard to leave on shore!"

The Admiral walked slowly towards the door. To-day had aged him years. Then he turned and looked benignantly at Jacques de Wissant; the man before him might be stiff, cold, awkward in manner, but he was a gentleman, a man of honour.

And as he drove to the station to meet the Minister of Marine, Admiral de Saint Vilquier's shrewd, practical mind began to deal with the difficult problem which was now added to his other cares. It was simplified in view of the fact—the awful fact—that according to his private information it was most unlikely that the submarine would be raised within the next few hours. He hoped with all his heart that the twelve men and the woman now lying beneath the sea had met death at the moment of the collision.

All that summer night the cafés and eating-houses of Falaise remained open, and there was a constant coming and going to the beach, where many people, even among those visitors who were not directly interested in the calamity, camped out on the stones.

The mayor sent word to the Pavillon de

Wissant that he would sleep in his town house, but though he left the town hall at two in the morning he was back at his post by eight, and he spent there the whole of the next long dragging day.

Fortunately for him there was little time for thought. In addition to the messages of inquiry and condolence which went on pouring in, important members of the Government arrived from Paris and the provinces.

There also came to Falaise the mother of Commander Dupré, and the father and brother of Lieutenant Paritot. De Wissant made the latter his special care. They, the two men, were granted the relief of tears, but Madame Dupré's silent agony could not be assuaged.

Once, when he suddenly came upon her sitting, her chin in her hand, in his room at the town hall, Jacques de Wissant shrank from her blazing eyes and ravaged face, so vividly did they recall to him the eyes, the face, he had seen that April evening "'twixt dog and wolf," when he had first leapt upon the truth.

On the third day all hope that there could be anyone still living in the *Neptune* was being abandoned, and yet at noon there ran a rumour through the town that knocking had been heard in the submarine. . . .

The mayor himself drew up an official proclamation, in which it was pointed out that it was almost certain that all on board had perished at the time of the collision, and that, even if any of them had survived for a few hours, not one could be alive now.

And then, as one by one the days of waiting began to wear themselves away, the world, apart from the town which numbered ten of her sons among the doomed men, relaxed its painful interest in the fate of the French submarine. Indeed, Falaise took on an almost winter stillness of aspect, for the summer visitors naturally drifted away from a spot which was still the heart of an awful tragedy.

But Jacques de Wissant did not relax in his duties or in his efforts on behalf of the families of the men who still lay, eighteen fathoms deep, encased in their steel tomb; and the townspeople were deeply moved by their mayor's continued, if restrained, distress. He even put his children, his pretty twin daughters, Jacqueline and Clairette, into deep mourning; this touched the seafaring portion of the population very much.

It also became known that M. de Wissant was suffering from domestic distress of a very sad and intimate kind; his sister-in-law was seriously ill in Italy from an infectious disease, and his wife, who had gone away at a moment's notice to help to nurse her, had caught the infection.

The Mayor of Falaise and Admiral de Saint Vilquier did not often have occasion to meet during those days spent by each of them in entertaining official personages and in composing answers to the messages and inquiries which went on dropping in, both by day and by night, at the town hall and at the Admiral's quarters. But there came an hour when Admiral de Saint Vilquier at last sought to have a private word with the Mayor of Falaise.

"I think I have arranged everything satisfactorily," he said briefly, "and you can convey the fact to your friends. I do not suppose, as matters are now, that there is much fear that the truth will ever come out."

The old man did not look into Jacques de Wissant's face while he uttered the comforting words. He had become aware of many things—including Madeleine Baudoin's cruise in the *Neptune* the day before the accident, and of her own and Claire de Wissant's reported departure for Italy.

Alone, among the people who sometimes had friendly speech of the mayor during those sombre days of waiting, Admiral de Saint Vilquier did not condole with the anxious husband on the fact that he could not yet leave Falaise for Mantua.

V

Jacques de Wissant woke with a start and sat up in bed. He had heard a knock—but, awake or sleeping, his ears were never free of the sound of knocking,—of muffled, regular knocking. . . .

It was the darkest hour of the summer night, but with a sharp sense of relief he became aware that what had wakened him this time was a real sound, not the slow, patient, rhythmical, tapping which haunted him incessantly. But now the knocking had been followed by the opening of his bedroom door, and vaguely outlined before him was the short, squat form of an old woman who had entered his mother's service when he was a little boy, and who always stayed in his town house.

"M'sieur l'Amiral de Saint Vilquier desires to see M'sieur Jacques on urgent business," she whispered. "I have put him to wait in the great drawing-room. It is fortunate that I took all the covers off the furniture yesterday."

Then the moment of ordeal, the moment he had begun to think would never come—was upon him? He knew this summons to mean that the *Neptune* had been finally towed into the harbour, and that now, in this still, dark hour before dawn, was about to begin the work of taking out the bodies.

Every day for a week past it had been publicly announced that the following night would see the final scene of the dread drama, and each evening—even last evening—it had been as publicly announced that nothing could be done for the present.

Jacques de Wissant had put all his trust in the Admiral and in the arrangements the Admiral was making to avoid discovery. But now, as he got up and dressed himself—strange to say that phantom sound of knocking had ceased—there came over him a frightful sensation of doubt and fear. Had he been right to trust wholly to the old naval officer? Would it not have been better to have taken the Minister of Marine into his confidence?

How would it be possible for Admiral de Saint Vilquier, unless backed by Governmental authority, to elude the vigilance, not only of the Admiralty officials and of all those that were directly interested, but also of the journalists who, however much the public interest had slackened in the disaster, still stayed on at Falaise in order to be present at the last act of the tragedy?

These thoughts jostled each other in Jacques de Wissant's brain. But whether he had been right or wrong it was too late to alter now.

He went into the room where the Admiral stood waiting for him.

The two men shook hands, but neither spoke till they had left the house. Then, as they walked with firm, quick steps across the deserted market-place, the Admiral said suddenly, "This is the quietest hour in the twenty-four, and though I anticipate a little trouble with the journalists, I think everything will go off quite well."

His companion muttered a word of assent, and the other went on, this time in a gruff whisper: "By the way, I have had to tell Dr. Tarnier—" and as Jacques de Wissant gave vent to a stifled exclamation of dismay— "of course I had to tell Dr. Tarnier! He has most nobly offered to go down into the *Neptune* alone—though in doing so he will run considerable personal risk."

Admiral de Saint Vilquier paused a moment,

for the quick pace at which his companion was walking made him rather breathless. "I have simply told him that there was a young woman on board. He imagines her to have been a Parisienne,—a person of no importance, you understand,—who had come to spend the holiday with poor Dupré. But he quite realizes that the fact must never be revealed." He spoke in a dry, matter-of-fact tone. "There will not be room on the pontoon for more than five or six, including ourselves and Dr. Tarnier. Doubtless some of our newspaper friends will be disappointed—if one can speak of disappointment in such a connection—but they will have plenty of opportunities of being present to-morrow and the following nights. I have arranged with the Minister of Marine for the work to be done only at night."

As the two men emerged on the quays, they saw that the news had leaked out, for knots of people stood about, talking in low hushed tones, and staring at the middle of the harbour.

Apart from the others, and almost dangerously close to the unguarded edge below which was the dark lapping water, stood a line of women shrouded in black, and from them came no sound.

As the Admiral and his companion approached the little group of officials who were apparently waiting for them, the old naval officer whispered to Jacques de Wissant, using for the first time the familiar expression, "*mon ami*," "Do not forget, *mon ami*, to thank the harbour-master and the pilot. They have had a very difficult task, and they will expect your commendation."

Jacques de Wissant said the words required of him. And then, at the last moment, just as he was on the point of going down the steps leading to the flat-bottomed boat in which they were to be rowed to the pontoon, there arose an angry discussion. The harbour-master had, it seemed, promised the representatives of two Paris newspapers that they should be present when the submarine was first opened.

But the Admiral stiffly asserted his supreme authority. "In such matters I can allow no favouritism! It is doubtful if any bodies will be taken out to-night, gentlemen, for the tide is already turning. I will see if other arrangements can be made to-morrow. If any of you had been in the harbour of Bizerta when the *Lutin* was raised, you would now thank me for not allowing you to view the sight which we may be about to see."

And the weary, disappointed special correspondents, who had spent long days watching for this one hour, realized that they would have to content themselves with describing what could be seen from the quays.

It will, however, surprise no one familiar with the remarkable enterprise of the modern press, when it is recorded that by far the most accurate account of what occurred during the hour that followed was written by a cosmopolitan war correspondent, who had had the good fortune of making Dr. Tarnier's acquaintance during the dull fortnight of waiting.

He wrote:

None of those who were there will ever forget what they saw last night in the harbour of Falaise.

The scene, illumined by the searchlight of a destroyer, was at once sinister, sombre, and magnificent. Below the high, narrow pontoon, on the floor of the harbour, lay the wrecked submarine; and those who gazed down at the *Neptune* felt as though they were in the presence of what had once been a sentient being done to death by some huge Goliath of the deep.

Dr. Tarnier, the chief medical officer of the port—a man who is beloved and respected by the whole population of Falaise—stood ready to begin his dreadful task. I had ascertained that he had obtained permission to go down alone into the hold of death—an exploration attended with the utmost physical risk.

He was clad in a suit of india-rubber clothing, and over his arm was folded a large tarpaulin sheet lined with carbolic wool, one of half a dozen such sheets lying at his feet.

The difficult work of unsealing the conning tower was then proceeded with in the presence of Admiral de Saint Vilquier, whose prowess as a midshipman is still remembered by British Crimean veterans— and of the Mayor of Falaise, M. Jacques de Wissant.

At last there came a guttural exclamation of "Ça y est!" and Dr. Tarnier stepped downwards, to emerge a moment later with the first body, obviously that of the gallant Commander Dupré, who was found, as it was expected he would be, in the conning tower.

Once more the doctor's burly figure disappeared, once more he emerged, tenderly bearing a slighter, lighter burden, obviously the boyish form of Lieutenant Paritot, who was found close to Commander Dupré.

The tide was rising rapidly, but two more bodies— this time with the help of a webbed band cleverly designed by Dr. Tarnier with a view to the purpose —were lifted from the inner portion of the submarine.

The four bodies, rather to the disappointment of the large crowd which had gradually gathered on the quays, were not taken directly to the shore, to the great hall where Falaise is to mourn her dead sons; one by one they were reverently conveyed, by the Admiral's orders, to a barge which was once used as a hospital ward for sick sailors, and which is close to the mouth of the harbour. Thence, when all twelve bodies have been recovered—that is, in three or four days, for the work is only to be proceeded with at night,—they will be taken to the Salle d'Armes, there to await the official obsequies.

On the morning following the night during which the last body was lifted from within the *Neptune*, there ran a curious rumour through the fishing quarter of the town. It was said that thirteen bodies—not twelve, as declared the official report—had been taken out of the *Neptune*. It was declared on the authority of one of the seamen—a Gascon, be it noted—who had been there on that first night, that five, not four, bodies had been conveyed to the hospital barge.

But the rumour, though it found an echo in the French press, was not regarded as worth an official denial, and it received its final quietus on the day of the official obsequies, when it was at once seen that the number of ammunition wagons heading the great procession was twelve.

As long as tradition endures in the life of the town, Falaise will remember the *Neptune* funeral procession. Not only was every navy in the world represented, but also every strand of that loosely woven human fabric we civilized peoples call a nation.

Through the long line of soldiers, each man with his arms reversed, walked the official mourners, while from the fortifications there boomed the minute gun.

First the President of the French Republic, with, to his right, the Minister of Marine; and close behind them the stiff, still vigorous, figure of old Admiral de Saint Vilquier. By his side walked the Mayor of Falaise—so mortally pale, so what the French call undone, that the Admiral felt fearful lest his neighbour should be compelled to fall out.

But Jacques de Wissant was not minded to fall out.

The crowd looking on, especially the wives of those substantial citizens of the town who stood at their windows behind half-closed shutters and drawn blinds, stared down at the mayor with pitying concern.

"He has a warm heart though a cold manner," murmured these ladies to one another, "and just now, you know, he is in great anxiety, for his wife—that beautiful Claire with whom he doesn't get on very well—is in Italy, seriously ill of scarlet fever." "Yes, and as soon as this sad ceremony is over, he will leave for the south—I hear that the President has offered him a seat in his saloon as far as Paris."

As the head of the procession at last stopped on the great parade ground where the last honours were to be rendered to the lowly yet illustrious dead, Jacques de Wissant straightened himself with an instinctive gesture, and his lips began to move. He was muttering to himself the speech he would soon have to deliver, and which he had that morning, making a great mental effort, committed to memory.

And after the President had had his long, emotional, and flowery say; and when the oldest of French admirals had stepped forward and, in a quavering voice, bidden the dead farewell on behalf of the Navy, it came to the turn of the Mayor of Falaise.

He was there, he said, simply as the mouthpiece of his fellow-townsmen, and they, bowed as they were by deep personal grief, could say but little—they could indeed only murmur their eternal gratitude for the sympathy they had received, and were now receiving, from their countrymen and from the world.

Then Jacques de Wissant gave a brief personal account of each of the ten seamen whom this vast concourse had gathered together to honour. It was noted by the curious in such things that he made no allusion to the two officers, to Commander Dupré and Lieutenant

Paritot ; doubtless he thought that they, after all, had been amply honoured in the preceding speeches.

But though his care for the lowly heroes proved the Mayor of Falaise a good republican, he showed himself in the popular estimation also a scholar, for he wound up with the old tag—the grand old tag which inspired so many noble souls in the proudest of ancient empires and civilizations, and which will retain the power of moving and thrilling generations yet unborn in both the Western and the Eastern worlds :

"Dulce et decorum est pro patria mori."

THE CHILD

THE CHILD

I

IT was close on eleven o'clock; the July night was airless, and the last of that season's great balls was taking place in Grosvenor Square.

Mrs. Elwyn's brougham came to a sudden halt in Green Street. Encompassed behind and before with close, intricate traffic, the carriage swung stiffly on its old-fashioned springs, responding to every movement of the fretted horse.

Hugh Elwyn, sitting by his mother's side, wondered a little impatiently why she remained so faithful to the old brougham which he could remember, or so it seemed to him, all his life. But he did not utter his thoughts aloud; he still went in awe of his mother, and he was proud, in a whimsical way, of her old-fashioned austerity of life, of her narrowness of vision, of her dislike of modern ways and new fashions.

Mrs. Elwyn after her husband's death had

given up the world. This was the first time since her widowhood that she and her son had dined out together; but then the occasion was a very special one—they had been to dinner with the family of Elwyn's fiancée, Winifred Fanshawe.

Hugh Elwyn turned and looked at his mother. As he saw in the half-darkness the outlines of the delicately pure profile, framed in grey bands of hair covering the ears as it had been worn when Mrs. Elwyn was a girl upwards of forty years ago, he felt stirred with an unwonted tenderness, added to the respect with which he habitually regarded her.

Since leaving Cavendish Square they had scarcely spoken the one to the other. The drive home was a short one, for they lived in South Street. It was tiresome that they should be held up in this way within a hundred yards of their own door.

Suddenly the mother spoke. She put out her frail hand and laid it across her son's strong brown fingers. She gazed earnestly into the good-looking face which was not as radiantly glad as she would have wished to see it—as indeed she had once seen her son's face look, and as she could still very vividly remember her own husband's face had looked during their short formal engagement nearly fifty years ago. "I could not be better pleased, Hugh, if I had myself chosen your future wife."

Elwyn was a little amused as well as touched; he was well aware that his mother, to all intents and purposes, *had* chosen Winifred. True, she had been but slightly acquainted with the girl before the engagement, but she had "known all about her," and had been on terms of friendly acquaintance with Winifred's grandmother all her long life. Elwyn remembered how his mother had pressed him to accept an invitation to a country house where Winifred Fanshawe was to be. But Mrs. Elwyn had never spoken to her son of her wishes until the day he had come and told her that he intended to ask Winifred to marry him, and then her unselfish joy had moved him and brought them very near to one another.

When Hugh Elwyn was in London—he had been a great wanderer over the earth—he lived with his mother, and they were outwardly on the closest, most intimate terms of affection. But then Mrs. Elwyn never interfered with Hugh, as he understood his friends' mothers so often interfered with them and with their private affairs. This doubtless was why they were, and remained, on such ideal terms together.

Suddenly Mrs. Elwyn again spoke, but she

did not turn round and look tenderly at her son as she had done when speaking of his future wife—this time she gazed straight before her: "Is not Winifred a cousin of Mrs. Bellair?"

"Yes, there's some kind of connection between the Fanshawes and the Bellairs."

Hugh Elwyn tried to make his voice unconcerned, but he failed, and he knew that he had failed. His mother's question had disturbed him, and taken him greatly by surprise.

"I wondered whether they are friends?"

"I have never heard Winifred mention her," he said shortly. "Yes, I have—I remember now that she told me the Bellairs had sent her a present the very day after our engagement was in the *Morning Post*."

"Then I suppose you will have to see something of them after your marriage?"

"You mean the Bellairs? Yes—no. I don't think that follows, mother."

"Do you see anything of them now?"

"No"—he again hesitated, and again ate his word—"that is—yes. I met them some weeks ago. But I don't think we are likely to see much of them after our marriage."

He would have given the world to feel that

his voice was betraying nothing of the discomfort he was feeling.

"I hope not, Hugh. Mrs. Bellair would not be a suitable friend for Winifred—or—or for any young married woman."

"Mother!" Elwyn only uttered the one word, but anger, shame, and self-reproach were struggling in the tone in which he uttered that one word. "You are wrong, indeed, you are quite wrong—I mean about Fanny Bellair."

"My dear," she said gently, but her voice quivered, "I do not think I am wrong. Indeed, I know I am right." Neither had ever seen the other so moved. "My dear," again she said the two quiet words that may mean so much or so little, "you know that I never spoke to you of the matter. I tried never even to think of it, and yet, Hugh, it made me very anxious, very unhappy. But to-night, looking at that sweet girl, I felt I must speak."

She waited a moment, and then added in a constrained voice, "I do not judge you, Hugh."

"No!" he cried, "but you judge her! And it's so unfair, mother—so horribly unfair!"

He had turned round; he was forcing his mother to look at his now moody, unhappy face.

Mrs. Elwyn shrank back and closed her lips tightly. Her expression recalled to her son the look which used to come over her face when, as a petted, over cared-for only child, he asked her for something which she believed it would he bad for him to have. From that look there had been, in old days, no appeal. But now he felt that he must say something more. His manhood demanded it of him.

"Mother," he said earnestly, "as you have spoken to me of the matter, I feel I must have it out with you! Please believe me when I say that you are being unjust—indeed, cruelly so. I was to blame all through—from the very beginning to the very end."

"You must allow me," she said in a low tone, "to be the judge of that, Hugh." She added deprecatingly, "This discussion is painful, and—and very distasteful to me."

Her son leant back, and choked down the words he was about to utter. He knew well that nothing he could say would change or even modify his mother's point of view. But oh! why had she done this? Why had she chosen to-night, of all nights, to rend the veil which had always hung, so decently, between them. He had felt happy to-night—not madly, foolishly happy, as so many men feel at such moments, but reasonably, decorously pleased with his present and his future. He was making a *mariage de convenance*, but there had been another man on the lists, a younger man than himself, and that had added a most pleasing zest to the pursuit. He, aided of course by Winifred Fanshawe's prudent parents, had won—won a very pretty, well-bred, well-behaved girl to wife. What more could a man of forty-one, who had lived every moment of his life, ask of that providence which shapes our ends?

The traffic suddenly parted, and the horse leapt forward.

As they reached their own front door, Mrs. Elwyn again spoke: "Perhaps I ought to add," she said hurriedly, "that I know one thing to Mrs. Bellair's credit. I am told that she is a most devoted and careful mother to that little boy of hers. I heard to-day that the child is seriously ill, and that she and the child's nurse are doing everything for him."

Mrs. Elwyn's voice had softened, curiously. She had an old-fashioned prejudice against trained nurses.

Hugh Elwyn helped his mother into the house; then, in the hall, he bent down and just touched her cheek with his lips.

"Won't you come up into the drawing-room? Just for a few minutes?" she asked;

there was a note of deep, yearning disappointment in her voice, and her face looked grey and tired, very different from the happy, placid air it had worn during the little dinner party.

"No, thank you, mother, I won't come up just now. I think I'll go out again for half an hour. I haven't walked at all to-day, and it's so hot—I feel I shouldn't sleep if I turn in now."

He was punishing his mother as he had seen other sons punishing their mothers, but as he himself had never before to-night been tempted to punish his. Nay, more, as Hugh Elwyn watched her slow ascent up the staircase, he told himself that she had hurt and angered him past entire forgiveness. He had sometimes suspected that she knew of that fateful episode in his past life, but he had never supposed that she would speak of it to him, especially not now, after years had gone by, and when, greatly to please her, he was about to make what is called a "suitable" marriage.

He was just enough to know that his mother had hurt herself by hurting him, but that did not modify his feelings of anger and of surprise at what she had done. Of course she thought she knew everything there was to know, but how much there had been that she had never even suspected!

Those words—that admission—as to Fanny Bellair being a good mother would never have passed Mrs. Elwyn's lips—they would never even have been credited by her had she known the truth—the truth, that is, as to the child to whom Mrs. Bellair was so passionately devoted, and who now, it seemed, was ailing. That secret, and Hugh Elwyn thanked God, not irreverently, that it was so, was only shared by two human beings, that is by Fanny and himself. And perhaps, Fanny, like himself, had managed by now almost to forget it. . . .

Elwyn swung out of the house, he walked up South Street, and so into Park Lane and over to the Park railings. There was still a great deal of traffic in the roadway, but the pavements were deserted.

As he began to walk quickly westward, the past came back and overwhelmed him as with a great flood of mingled memories. And it was not, as his mother would probably have visioned it, a muddy spate filled with unclean things. Rather was it a flood of exquisite spring waters, instinct with the buoyant headlong rushes of youth, and filled with clear, happy shallows, in which retrospectively he lay and sunned himself in the warmth of what had been a great love—love such as Winifred Fanshawe, with her thin, complaisant nature, would never bestow.

The mother's imprudent words of unnecessary warning had brought back to her son everything she had hoped was now, if not obliterated, then repented of; but Elwyn's heart was filled to-night with a vague tenderness for the half-forgotten woman whom he had loved awhile with so passionate and absorbing a love, and to whom, under cover of that poor and wilted thing, his conscience, he had ultimately behaved so ill.

Hugh Elwyn's mind travelled back across the years, to the very beginning of his involved account with honour—that account which he believed to be now straightened out.

Jim Bellair had been Elwyn's friend—first college friend and then favourite "pal." When Bellair had fallen head over ears in love with a girl still in the schoolroom, a girl not even pretty, but with wonderful auburn hair and dark, startled-looking eyes, and had finally persuaded, cajoled, badgered her into saying "Yes," it was Hugh Elwyn who had been Bellair's rather sulky best man. Small wonder that the bridegroom had half-jokingly left his young wife in Elwyn's charge when he had had to go half across the world on business that could not be delayed, while she stayed behind to nurse her father who was ill.

It was then, with mysterious, uncanny suddenness, that the mischief had begun. There had been something wild and untamed in Fanny Bellair — something which had roused in Elwyn the hunter's instinct, an instinct hitherto unslaked by over easy victories. And then Chance, that great, cynical goddess which plays so great a part in civilized life, had flung first one opportunity and then another into his eager, grasping hands.

Fanny's father had died; and she had been lonely and in sorrow. Careless friends, however kind, do not care to see much of those who mourn, but he, Hugh Elwyn, had not been careless, nay, he had been careful to see more, not less, of his friend's wife in this her first great grief, and she had been moved to the heart by his sympathy.

It was by Elwyn's advice that Mrs. Bellair had taken a house not far from London that lovely summer.

Ah, that little house! Elwyn could remember every bush, almost every flower that had flowered, in the walled garden during those enchanted weeks. Against the background of his mind every ornament, every odd piece of furniture in that old cottage, stood out as having been the silent, it had seemed at the time the kindly, understanding witnesses of what had by then become an exquisite friendship. He, the man, had known almost from the first where they too were drifting, but she, the woman, had slipped into love as a wanderer at night slips suddenly into a deep and hidden pool.

In a story book they would both have gone away openly together — but somehow the thought of doing such a thing never seriously occurred to Elwyn. He was far too fond of Bellair—it seemed absurd to say that now, but the truth, especially the truth of what has been, is often absurd.

Elwyn had contented himself with stealing Bellair's wife; he had no desire to put public shame and ridicule upon his friend. And fortune, favouring him, had prolonged the other man's enforced absence.

And then? And then at last Bellair had come back,—and trouble began. As to many things, nay, as to most things which have to do with the flesh rather than the spirit, men are more fastidiously delicate than are women. There had come months of misery, of revolt, and, on Elwyn's part, of dulling love. . . .

Then, once more, Chance gave him an unlooked-for opportunity—an opportunity of escape from what had become to him an intolerable position.

The war broke out, and Hugh Elwyn was among the very first of those gallant fellows who volunteered during the dark November of '99.

By a curious irony of fate, the troopship that bore him to South Africa had Bellair also on board, but owing to Elwyn's secret decision—he was far the cleverer man of the two—he and his friend were no longer bound together by that wordless intimacy which is the basis of any close tie among men. By the time the two came back from Africa they had become little more than cordial acquaintances. Marriage, so Bellair sometimes told himself ruefully, generally plays the devil with a man's bachelor friendships. He was a kindly, generous hearted soul, who found much comfort in platitudes. . . .

But that, alas! had not been the end. On Elwyn's return home there had come to him a violent, overmastering revival of his passion. Again he and Fanny met—again they loved. Then one terrible day she came and told him, with stricken eyes, what he sometimes hoped, even now, had not been true—that she was about to have a child, and that it would be his child. At that moment, as he knew well, Mrs. Bellair had desired ardently to go away with him, openly. But he had drawn back, assuring himself—and this time honestly—that his shrinking from that course, now surely the only honest course, was not wholly ignoble. Were he to do such a thing it would go far to kill his mother—worse, it would embitter every moment of the life which remained to her.

For a while Elwyn went in deadly fear lest Fanny should tell her husband the truth. But the weeks and months drifted by, and she remained silent. And as he had gone about that year, petted and made much of by his friends and acquaintances—for did he not bear on his worn, handsome face that look which war paints on the face of your sensitive modern man?—he heard whispered the delightful news that after five years of marriage kind Jim and dear Fanny Bellair were at last going to be made happy—happy in the good old way.

Among the other memories of that hateful time, one came back, to-night, with especial vividness. Hurrying home across the park one afternoon, seven years ago now, almost to a day, he had suddenly run up against Bellair.

They had talked for a few moments on indifferent things, and then Jim had said shyly, awkwardly, but with a beaming look on his face, "You know about Fanny? Of course I can't help feeling a bit anxious, but she's so healthy—not like those women who have always something the matter with them!" And he, Elwyn, had gripped the other man's hand, and muttered the congratulation which was being asked of him.

That meeting, so full of shameful irony, had occurred about a week before the child's birth. Elwyn had meant to be away from London— but Chance, so carelessly kind a friend to him in the past, at last proved cruel, for surely it was Chance and Chance alone that led him, on the very eve of the day he was starting for Norway, straight across the quiet square, composed of high Georgian houses, where the Bellairs still lived.

To-night, thanks to his mother, every incident of that long, agonizing night came back. He could almost feel the tremor of half fear, half excitement, which had possessed him when he had suddenly become aware that his friends' house was still lit up and astir, and that fresh straw lay heaped up in prodigal profusion in the road where, a little past the door, was drawn up a doctor's one-horse brougham. Even then he might have taken another way, but something had seemed to drive him on, past the house,—and there Elwyn, staying his deadened footsteps, had heard float down to him from widely opened windows above, certain sounds, muffled moans, telling of a physical extremity which even now he winced to remember.

He had waited on and on—longing to escape, and yet prisoned between imaginary bounds within which he paced up and down, filled with an obscure desire to share, in the measure that was possible to him, her torment.

At last, in the orange, dust-laden dawn of a London summer morning, the front door of the house had opened, and Elwyn had walked forward, every nerve quivering with suspense and fatigue, feeling that he must know. . . .

A great doctor, with whose face he was vaguely acquainted, had stepped out accompanied by Bellair—Bellair with ruffled hair and red-rimmed eyes, but looking if tired then content, even more, triumphant. Elwyn had heard him say the words, "Thanks awfully. I shall never forget how kind you have been, Sir Joseph. Yes, I'll go to bed at once. I know you must have thought me rather stupid."

And then Bellair had suddenly seen Elwyn standing on the pavement; he had accepted unquestioningly the halting explanation that he was on his way home from a late party, and had happened, as it were, that way. "It's a boy!" he had said exultantly, although Elwyn had asked him no question, and then, "Of course I'm awfully pleased, but I'm dog tired! She's had a bad time, poor girl—but it's all right now, thank God! Come in and have a drink, Hugo."

But Elwyn had shaken his head. Again he had gripped his old friend's hand, as he had done a week before, and again he had muttered the necessary words of congratulation. Then, turning on his heel, he had gone home, and spent the rest of the night in desultory packing.

That was just seven years ago, and Elwyn had never seen Fanny's child. He had been away from England for over a year, and when he came back he learned that the Bellairs were away, living in the country, where they had taken a house for the sake of their boy.

As time had gone on, Elwyn and his friends had somehow drifted apart, as people are apt to drift apart in the busy idleness of the life led by the fortunate Bellairs and Elwyns of this world. Fanny avoided Hugh Elwyn, and Elwyn avoided Fanny, but they two only were aware of this. It was the last of the many secrets which they had once shared. When he and Bellair by chance met alone, all the old cordiality and even the old affection seemed to come back, if not to Elwyn then to the other man.

And now the child, to whom it seemed not only Fanny but Jim Bellair also was so devoted, was ill, and he, Hugh Elwyn, had been the last to hear of it. He felt vaguely remorseful that this should be so. There had been years when nothing that affected Bellair could have left him indifferent, and a time when the slightest misadventure befalling Fanny would have called forth his eager, helpful sympathy.

How strange it would be—he quickened his footsteps—if this child, with whom he was at once remotely and intimately concerned, were to die! He could not help feeling, deep down in his heart, that this would be, if a tragic, then a natural solution of a painful and unnatural problem—and then, quite suddenly, he felt horribly ashamed of having allowed himself to think this thought, to wish this awful wish.

Why should he not go now, at once, to Manchester Square, and inquire as to the little boy's condition? It was not really late, not yet midnight. He could go and leave a message, perhaps even scribble a line to Jim Bellair explaining that he had come round as soon as he had heard of the child's illness.

II

When Hugh Elwyn reached the familiar turning whence he could see the Bellairs' high house, time seemed to have slipped back.

The house was all lit up as it had been on that summer night seven years ago. Everything was the same—even to the heaped-up straw into which his half-reluctant feet now sank. There was even a doctor's carriage drawn up a little way from the front door, but this time it was a smart electric brougham.

He rang the bell, and as the door opened, Jim Bellair suddenly came into the hall, out of a room which Elwyn knew to be the smoking-room—a room in which he and Fanny had at one time spent long hours in contented, nay in ecstatic, dual solitude.

"I have come to inquire—I only heard to-night—" he began awkwardly, but the other cut him short, "Yes, yes, I understand—it's awfully good of you, Elwyn! I'm awfully glad to see you. Come in here—" and perforce he had to follow. "The doctor's upstairs —I mean Sir Joseph Pixton. Fanny was determined to have him, and he very kindly came, though of course he's not a child's doctor. He's annoyed because Fanny won't have trained nurses; but I don't suppose anything would make any difference. It's just a fight—a fight for the little chap's life—that's what it is, and we don't know yet who'll win."

He spoke in quick, short sentences, staring with widely open eyes at his erstwhile friend as he spoke. "Pneumonia—I suppose you don't know anything about it? I thought children never had such things, especially not in hot weather."

"I had a frightful illness when I was about your boy's age," said Elwyn eagerly. "It's the first thing I can really remember. They called it inflammation of the lungs. I was awfully bad. My mother talks of it now, sometimes."

"Does she?" Bellair spoke wearily. "If only one could *do* something," he went on. "But you see the worst of it is that I can do nothing—nothing! Fanny hates my being up there—she thinks it upsets the boy. He's such a jolly little chap, Hugo. You know we called him Peter after Fanny's father?"

Elwyn moved towards the door. He felt dreadfully moved by the other's pain. He told himself that after all he could do no good by staying, and he felt so ashamed, such a cur——

"You don't want to go away yet?" There was sharp chagrin, reproachful dismay, in Bellair's voice. Elwyn remembered that in old days Jim had always hated being alone. "Won't you stay and hear what Pixton says? Or—or are you in a hurry?"

Elwyn turned round. "Of course I'll stay," he said briefly.

Bellair spared him thanks, but he began walking about the room restlessly. At last he went to the door and set it ajar. "I want to hear when Sir Joseph comes down," he explained, and even as he spoke there came the sound of heavy, slow footsteps on the staircase.

Bellair went out and brought the great man in.

"I've told Mrs. Bellair that we ought to have Bewdley! He knows a great deal more about children than I can pretend to do; and I propose, with your leave, to go off now, myself, and if possible bring him back." The old doctor's keen eyes wandered as he spoke from Bellair's fair face to Hugh Elwyn's dark one. "Perhaps," he said, "perhaps, Mr. Bellair, you would get someone to telephone to Dr. Bewdley's house to say that I'm coming? It might save a few moments."

As Bellair left the room, the doctor turned

to Elwyn and said abruptly, "I hope you'll be able to stay with your brother? All this is very hard on him; Mrs. Bellair will scarcely allow him into the child's room, and though that, of course, is quite right, I'm sorry for the man. He's wrapped up in the child."

And when Bellair came back from accompanying the old doctor to his carriage, there was a smile on his face—the first smile which had been there for a long time: "Pixton thinks you're my brother! He said, 'I hope your brother will manage to stay with you for a bit.' Now I'll go up and see Fanny. Pixton is certainly more hopeful than the last man we had—"

Bellair's voice had a confident ring. Elwyn remembered with a pang that Jim had always been like that—always believed, that is, that the best would come to pass.

When left alone, Elwyn began walking restlessly up and down, much as his friend had walked up and down a few minutes ago. Something of the excitement of the fight going on above had entered into him; he now desired ardently that the child should live, should emerge victor from the grim struggle.

At last Bellair came back. "Fanny believes that this is the night of crisis," he said slowly. All the buoyancy had left his voice. "But—

but Elwyn, I hope you won't mind—the fact is she's set her heart on your seeing him. I told her what you told me about yourself, I mean your illness as a child, and it's cheered her up amazingly, poor girl! Perhaps you could tell her a little bit more about it, though I like to think that if the boy gets through it"—his voice broke suddenly—"she won't remember this—this awful time. But don't let's keep her waiting—" He took Elwyn's consent for granted, and quickly the two men walked up the stairs of the high house, on and on and on.

"It's a good way up," whispered Bellair, "but Fanny was told that a child's nursery couldn't be too high. So we had the four rooms at the top thrown into two."

They were now on the dimly-lighted landing. "Wait one moment — wait one moment, Hugo." Bellair's voice had dropped to a low, gruff whisper.

Elwyn remained alone. He could hear slight movements going on in the room into which Bellair had just gone; and then there also fell on his ears the deep, regular sound of snoring. Who could be asleep in the house at such a moment? The sound disturbed him; it seemed to add a touch of grotesque horror to the situation.

Suddenly the handle of the door in front of him moved round, and he heard Fanny Bellair's voice, unnaturally controlled and calm. "I sent Nanna to bed, Jim. The poor old creature was absolutely worn out. And then I would so much rather be alone when Sir Joseph brings back the other doctor. He admits—I mean Sir Joseph does—that to-night *is* the crisis."

The door swung widely open, and Elwyn, moving instinctively back, visualized the scene before him very distinctly.

There was a screen on the right hand, a screen covered, as had been the one in his own nursery, with a patchwork of pictures varnished over.

Mrs. Bellair stood between the screen and the pale blue wall. Her slim figure was clad in some sort of long white garment, and over it she wore an apron, which he noticed was far too large for her. Her hair, the auburn hair which had been her greatest beauty, and which he had once loved to praise and to caress, was fastened back, massed up in as small a compass as possible. That, and the fact that her face was expressionless, so altered her in Elwyn's eyes as to give him an uncanny feeling that the woman before him was not the woman he had known, had loved, had left,—but a stranger, only bound to him by the slender link of a common humanity.

She waited some moments as if listening, then she came out on to the landing, and shut the door behind her very softly.

The sentence of conventional sympathy half formed on Elwyn's lips died into nothingness; as little could he have offered words of cheer to one who was being tortured; but in the dim light their hands met and clasped tightly.

"Hugo?" she said, "I want to ask you something. You told Jim just now that you were once very ill as a child,—ill like this, ill like my child. I want you to tell me honestly if that is true? I mean, were you very, very ill?"

He answered her in the same way, without preamble, baldly: "It is quite true," he said. "I was very ill—so ill that my mother for one moment thought that I was dead. But remember, Fanny, that in those days they did not know nearly as much as they do now. Your boy has two chances for every one that I had then."

"Would you mind coming in and seeing him?" Her voice faltered, it had become more human, more conventional, in quality.

"Of course I will see him," he said. "I

want to see him,—dear." She had suddenly become to him once more the thing nearest his heart; once more the link between them became of the closest, most intimate nature, and yet, or perhaps because of its intensity, the sense of nearness which had sprung at her touch into being was passionless.

The face which had been drained of all expression quickened into agonized feeling. She tried to withdraw her hand from his, but he held it firmly, and it was hand in hand that together they walked into the room.

As they came round the screen behind which lay the sick child, Bellair went over to the farthest of the three windows and stood there with crossed arms staring out into the night.

The little boy lay on his right side, and as they moved round to the edge of the large cot, Elwyn, with a sudden tightening of the throat, became aware that the child was neither asleep nor, as he in his ignorance had expected to find him, sunk in stupor or delirium. But the small, dark face, framed by the white pillow, was set in lines of deep, unchildlike gravity, and in the eyes which now gazed incuriously at Elwyn there was a strange, watchful light which seemed to illumine that which was within rather than that which was without.

As is always the case with a living creature

near to death, little Peter Bellair looked very lonely.

Then Elwyn, moving nearer still, seemed— or so at least Fanny Bellair will ever believe —to take possession of the moribund child, yielding him as he did so something of his own strength to help him through the crisis then imminent. And indeed the little creature whose forehead, whose clenched left hand lying on the sheet were beginning to glisten with sweat, appeared to become merged in some strange way with himself. Merged, not with the man he was to-day, but with the Hugh Elwyn of thirty years back, who, as a lonely only child, had lived so intensely secret, imaginative a life, peopling the prim alleys of Hyde Park with fairies, imps, tricksy hobgoblins in whom he more than half believed, and longing even then, as ever after, for the unattainable, never carelessly happy as his father and mother believed him to be. . . .

Hugh Elwyn stayed with the Bellairs all that night. He shared the sick suspense the hour of the crisis brought, and he was present when the specialist said the fateful words, "I think, under God, this child will live."

When at last Elwyn left the house, clad in an old light coat of Bellair's in order that the folk early astir should not see that he was wearing evening clothes, he felt happier, more light-hearted, than he had done for years.

His life had been like a crowded lumber-room, full of useless and worn-out things he had accounted precious, while he had ignored the one possession that really mattered and that linked him, not only with the future, but with the greatest reality of his past.

The inevitable pain which this suddenly discovered treasure was to bring was mercifully concealed from him, as also the sombre fact that he would henceforth go lonely all his life, perforce obliged to content himself with the crumbs of another man's feast. For Peter Bellair, high-strung, imaginative, as he will ever be, will worship the strong, kindly, simple man he believes to be his father, but to that dear father's friend he will only yield the careless affection born of gratitude for much kindness.

In the matter of the broken engagement, Hugh Elwyn was more fairly treated by the men and women whom the matter concerned, or who thought it concerned them, than are the majority of recusant lovers.

"Hugh Elwyn has never been quite the same since the war, and you know Winifred Fanshawe really liked the other man the best," so said those who spent an idle moment in discussing the matter, and they generally added, "It's a good thing that he's spending the summer with his old friends, the Bellairs. They're living very quietly just now, for their little boy has been dreadfully ill, so it's just the place for poor old Hugo to get over it all!"

ST. CATHERINE'S EVE

ST. CATHERINE'S EVE

1

"IN this matter of the railway James Mottram has proved a false friend, a very traitor to me!"

Charles Nagle's brown eyes shone with anger; he looked loweringly at his companions, and they, a beautiful young woman and an old man dressed in the sober garb of a Catholic ecclesiastic of that day, glanced at one another apprehensively.

All England was then sharply divided into two camps, the one composed of those who welcomed with enthusiasm the wonderful new invention which obliterated space, the other of those who dreaded and abhorred the coming of the railroads.

Charles Nagle got up and walked to the end of the terrace. He stared down into the wooded combe, or ravine, below, and noted with sullen anger the signs of stir and activity in the narrow strip of wood which till a few weeks before had been so still, so entirely remote from even the quiet human activities of 1835.

At last he turned round, pirouetting on his heel with a quick movement, and his good looks impressed anew each of the two who sat there with him. Eighty years ago beauty of line and colour were allowed to tell in masculine apparel, and this young Dorset squire delighted in fine clothes. Though November was far advanced it was a mild day, and Charles Nagle wore a bright blue coat, cut, as was then the fashion, to show off the points of his elegant figure—of his slender waist and his broad shoulders; as for the elaborately frilled waistcoat, it terminated in an India muslin stock, wound many times round his neck. He looked a foppish Londoner rather than what he was—an honest country gentleman who had not journeyed to the capital for some six years, and then only to see a great physician.

"'Twas a most unneighbourly act on the part of James—he knows it well enough, for we hardly see him now!" He addressed his words more particularly to his wife, and he spoke more gently than before.

The old priest—his name was Dorriforth—looked uneasily from his host to his hostess. He felt that both these young people, whom he had known from childhood, and whom he loved well, had altered during the few weeks which had gone by since he had last seen them. Rather—he mentally corrected himself—it was the wife, Catherine, who was changed. Charles Nagle was much the same; poor Charles would never be other, for he belonged to the mysterious company of those who, physically sound, are mentally infirm, and shunned by their more fortunate fellows.

But Charles Nagle's wife, the sweet young woman who for so long had been content, nay glad, to share this pitiful exile, seemed now to have escaped, if not in body then in mind, from the place where her sad, monotonous duty lay.

She did not at once answer her husband; but she looked at him fixedly, her hand smoothing nervously the skirt of her pretty gown.

Mrs. Nagle's dress also showed a care and research unusual in that of the country lady of those days. This was partly no doubt owing to her French blood—her grandparents had been *émigrés*—and to the fact that Charles liked to see her in light colours. The gown she was now wearing on this mild November day was a French flowered silk, the spoil of a smuggler who pursued his profitable calling on the coast hard by. The short, high bodice and puffed sleeves were draped with a scarf of Buckinghamshire lace which left, as was the fashion of those days, the wearer's lovely shoulders bare.

"James Mottram," she said at last, and with a heightened colour, "believes in progress, Charles. It is the one thing concerning which you and your friend will never agree."

"Friend?" he repeated moodily. "Friend! James Mottram has shown himself no friend of ours. And then I had rights in this matter —am I not his heir-at-law? I could prevent my cousin from touching a stone, or felling a tree, at the Eype. But 'tis his indifference to my feelings that angers me so. Why, I trusted the fellow as if he had been my brother!"

"And James Mottram," said the old priest authoritatively, "has always felt the same to you, Charles. Never forget that! In all but name you are brothers. Were you not brought up together? Had I not the schooling of you both as lads?" He spoke with a good deal of feeling; he had noticed—and the fact disturbed him—that Charles Nagle spoke in the past tense when referring to his affection for the absent man.

"But surely, sir, you cannot approve that

this iron monster should invade our quiet neighbourhood?" exclaimed Charles impatiently.

Mrs. Nagle looked at the priest entreatingly. Did she by any chance suppose that he would be able to modify her husband's violent feeling?

"If I am to say the truth, Charles," said Mr. Dorriforth mildly, "and you would not have me conceal my sentiments, then I believe the time will come when even you will be reconciled to this marvellous invention. Those who surely know declare that, thanks to these railroads, our beloved country will soon be all cultivated as is a garden. Nay, perhaps others of our Faith, strangers, will settle here——"

"Strangers?" repeated Charles Nagle sombrely, "I wish no strangers here. Even now there are too many strangers about." He looked round as if he expected those strangers of whom the priest had spoken to appear suddenly from behind the yew hedges which stretched away, enclosing Catherine Nagle's charming garden, to the left of the plateau on which stood the old manor-house.

"Nay, nay," he repeated, returning to his grievance, "never had I expected to find James Mottram a traitor to his order. As for the folk about here, they're bewitched! They believe that this puffing devil will make them all rich! I could tell them different; but, as you know, there are reasons why I should not."

The priest bent his head gravely. The Catholic gentry of those days were not on comfortable terms with their neighbours. In spite of the fact that legally they were now "emancipated," any malicious person could still make life intolerable to them. The railway mania was at its beginnings, and it would have been especially dangerous for Charles Nagle to take, in an active sense, the unpopular side.

In other parts of England, far from this Dorset countryside, railroads had brought with them a revival of trade. It was hoped that the same result would follow here, and a long strip of James Mottram's estate had been selected as being peculiarly suitable for the laying down of the iron track which was to connect the nearest town with the sea.

Unfortunately the land in question consisted of a wood which formed the boundary-line where Charles Nagle's property marched with that of his kinsman and co-religionist, James Mottram; and Nagle had taken the matter very ill indeed. He was now still suffering, in a physical sense, from the effects of the violent fit of passion which the matter had induced, and which even his wife, Catherine, had not been able to allay. . . .

As he started walking up and down with caged, impatient steps, she watched him with an uneasy, anxious glance. He kept shaking his head with a nervous movement, and he stared angrily across the ravine to the opposite hill, where against the skyline the large mass of Eype Castle, James Mottram's dwelling-place, stood four-square to the high winds which swept up from the sea.

Suddenly he again strode over to the edge of the terrace: "I think I'll go down and have a talk to those railroad fellows," he muttered uncertainly.

Charles knew well that this was among the forbidden things—the things he must not do; yet occasionally Catherine, who was, as the poor fellow dimly realized, his mentor and guardian, as well as his outwardly submissive wife, would allow him to do that which was forbidden.

But to-day such was not her humour. "Oh, no, Charles," she said decidedly, "you cannot go down to the wood! You must stay here and talk to Mr. Dorriforth."

"They were making hellish noises all last

night; I had no rest at all," Nagle went on inconsequently. "They were running their puffing devil up and down, 'The Bridport Wonder'—that's what they call it, reverend sir," he turned to the priest.

Catherine again looked up at her husband, and their old friend saw that she bit her lip as if checking herself in impatient speech. Was she losing the sweetness of her temper, the evenness of disposition the priest had ever admired in her, and even reverenced?

Mrs. Nagle knew that the steam-engine had been run over the line for the first time the night before, for James Mottram and she had arranged that the trial should take place then rather than in the daytime. She also knew that Charles had slept through the long dark hours, those hours during which she had lain wide awake by his side listening to the strange new sounds made by the Bridport Wonder. Doubtless one of the servants had spoken of the matter in his hearing.

She frowned, then felt ashamed. "Charles," she said gently, "would it not be well for me to go down to the wood and discover when these railroad men are going away? They say in the village that their work is now done."

"Yes," he cried eagerly. "A good idea,

love! And if they're going off at once, you might order that a barrel of good ale be sent down to them. I'm informed that that's what James has had done this very day. Now I've no wish that James should appear more generous than I!"

Catherine Nagle smiled, the indulgent kindly smile which a woman bestows on a loved child who suddenly betrays a touch of that vanity which is, in a child, so pardonable.

She went into the house, and in a few moments returned with a pink scarf wound about her soft dark hair—hair dressed high, turned back from her forehead in the old pre-Revolution French mode, and not, as was then the fashion, arranged in stiff curls.

The two men watched her walking swiftly along the terrace till she sank out of their sight, for a row of stone steps led down to an orchard planted with now leafless pear and apple trees, and surrounded with a quickset hedge. A wooden gate, with a strong lock to it, was set in this closely clipped hedge. It opened on a steep path which, after traversing two fields, terminated in the beech-wood where now ran the iron track of the new railroad.

Catherine Nagle unlocked the orchard gate, and went through on to the field path. And then she slackened her steps.

For hours, nay, for days, she had been longing for solitude, and now, for a brief space, solitude was hers. But, instead of bringing her peace, this respite from the companionship of Charles and of Mr. Dorriforth brought increased tumult and revolt.

She had ardently desired the visit of the old priest, but his presence had bestowed, instead of solace, fret and discomfort. When he fixed on her his mild, penetrating eyes, she felt as if he were dragging into the light certain secret things which had been so far closely hidden within her heart, and concerning which she had successfully dulled her once sensitive conscience.

The waking hours of the last two days had each been veined with torment. Her soul sickened as she thought of the morrow, St. Catherine's Day, that is, her feast-day. The *émigrés*, Mrs. Nagle's own people, had in exile jealousy kept up their own customs, and to Charles Nagle's wife the twenty-fifth day of November had always been a day of days, what her birthday is to a happy Englishwoman. Even Charles always remembered the date, and in concert with his faithful man-servant, Collins, sent to London each year for a pretty jewel. The housefolk, all of whom had learnt to love their mistress, and who helped her loyally in her difficult, sometimes perilous, task, also made of the feast a holiday.

But now, on this St. Catherine's Eve, Mrs. Nagle told herself that she was at the end of her strength. And yet only a month ago—so she now reminded herself piteously—all had been well with her; she had been strangely, pathetically happy a month since; content with all the conditions of her singular and unnatural life. . . .

Suddenly she stopped walking. As if in answer to a word spoken by an invisible companion she turned aside, and, stooping, picked a weed growing by the path. She held it up for a moment to her cheek, and then spoke aloud. "Were it not for James Mottram," she said slowly, and very clearly, "I, too, should become mad."

Then she looked round in sudden fear. Catherine Nagle had never before uttered, or permitted another to utter aloud in her presence, that awful word. But she knew that their neighbours were not so scrupulous. One cruel enemy, and, what was especially untoward, a close relation, Mrs. Felwake, own sister to Charles Nagle's dead father, often uttered it. This lady desired her son to reign at Edgecombe; it was she who in the last few years had spread abroad the notion that

Charles Nagle, in the public interest, should be asylumed.

In his own house, and among his own tenants, the slander was angrily denied. When Charles was stranger, more suspicious, moodier than usual, those about him would tell one another that "the squire was ill to-day," or that "the master was ailing." That he had a mysterious illness was admitted. Had not a famous London doctor persuaded Mr. Nagle that it would be dangerous for him to ride, even to walk outside the boundary of his small estate,—in brief, to run any risks which might affect his heart? He had now got out of the way of wishing to go far afield; contentedly he would pace up and down for hours on the long terrace which overhung the wood—talking, talking, talking, with Catherine on his arm.

But he was unselfish—sometimes. "Take a walk, dear heart, with James," he would say, and then Catherine Nagle and James Mottram would go out and make their way to some lonely farmhouse or cottage where Mottram had estate business. Yet during these expeditions they never forgot Charles, so Catherine now reminded herself sorely,—nay, it was then that they talked of him the most, discussing him kindly, tenderly, as they went. . . .

Catherine walked quickly on, her eyes on the ground. With a feeling of oppressed pain she recalled the last time she and Mottram had been alone together. Bound for a distant spot on the coast, they had gone on and on for miles, almost up to the cliffs below which lay the sea. Ah, how happy, how innocent she had felt that day!

Then they had come to a stile—Mottram had helped her up, helped her down, and for a moment her hand had lain and fluttered in his hand. . . .

During the long walk back, each had been very silent; and Catherine—she could not answer for her companion—when she had seen Charles waiting for her patiently, had felt a pained, shamed beat of the heart. As for James Mottram, he had gone home at once, scarce waiting for good-nights.

That evening—Catherine remembered it now with a certain comfort—she had been very kind to Charles; she was ever kind, but she had then been kinder than usual, and he had responded by becoming suddenly clearer in mind than she had known him to be for a long time. For some days he had been the old Charles—tender, whimsical, gallant, the Charles with whom, at a time when every girl is in love with love, she had alack! fallen in love. Then once more the cloud had come down, shadowing a dreary waste of days—dark days of oppression and of silence, alternating with sudden bursts of unreasonable and unreasoning rage.

James Mottram had come, and come frequently, during that time of misery. But his manner had changed. He had become restrained, as if watchful of himself; he was no longer the free, the happy, the lively companion he had used to be. Catherine scarcely saw him out of Charles's presence, and when they were by chance alone they talked of Charles, only of Charles and of his unhappy condition, and of what could be done to better it.

And now James Mottram had given up coming to Edgecombe in the old familiar way; or rather—and this galled Catherine shrewdly—he came only sufficiently often not to rouse remark among their servants and humble neighbours.

Catherine Nagle was on the edge of the wood, and looking about her she saw with surprise that the railway men she had come down to see had finished work for the day. There were signs of their immediate occupation, a fire was still smouldering, and the door of one of the shanties they occupied was open. But complete stillness reigned in this kingdom of high trees. To the right and left, as far as she could see, stretched the twin lines of rude iron rails laid down along what had been a cart-track, as well as a short cut between Edgecombe Manor and Eype Castle. A dun drift, to-day's harvest of dead leaves, had settled on the rails; even now it was difficult to follow their course.

As she stood there, about to turn and retrace her steps, Catherine suddenly saw James Mottram advancing quickly towards her, and the mingled revolt and sadness which had so wholly possessed her gave way to a sudden, overwhelming feeling of security and joy.

She moved from behind the little hut near which she had been standing, and a moment later they stood face to face.

James Mottram was as unlike Charles Nagle as two men of the same age, of the same breed, and of the same breeding could well be. He was shorter, and of sturdier build, than his cousin; and he was plain, whereas Charles Nagle was strikingly handsome. Also his face was tanned by constant exposure to sun, salt-wind, and rain; his hair was cut short, his face shaven.

The very clothes James Mottram wore were in almost ludicrous contrast to those which Charles Nagle affected, for Mottram's were always of serviceable homespun. But for the fact that they and he were scrupulously clean, the man now walking by Catherine Nagle's side might have been a prosperous farmer or bailiff instead of the owner of such large property in those parts as made him, in spite of his unpopular faith, lord of the little world about him.

On his plain face and strong, sturdy figure Catherine's beautiful eyes dwelt with unconscious relief. She was so weary of Charles's absorption in his apparel, and of his interest in the hundred and one fal-lals which then delighted the cosmopolitan men of fashion.

A simple, almost childish gladness filled her heart. Conscience, but just now so insistent and disturbing a familiar, vanished for a space, nay more, assumed the garb of a meddling busybody who seeks to discover harm where no harm is.

Was not James Mottram Charles's friend, almost, as the old priest had said, Charles's brother? Had she not herself deliberately chosen Charles in place of James when both young men had been in ardent pursuit of her

—James's pursuit almost wordless, Charles's conducted with all the eloquence of the poet he had then set out to be?

Mottram, seeing her in the wood, uttered a word of surprise. She explained her presence there. Their hands scarce touched in greeting, and then they started walking side by side up the field path.

Mottram carried a stout ash stick. Had the priest been there he would perchance have noticed that the man's hand twitched and moved restlessly as he swung his stick about; but Catherine only became aware that her companion was preoccupied and uneasy after they had gone some way.

When, however, the fact of his unease seemed forced upon her notice, she felt suddenly angered. There was a quality in Mrs. Nagle that made her ever ready to rise to meet and conquer circumstance. She told herself, with heightened colour, that James Mottram should and must return to his old ways—to his old familiar footing with her. Anything else would be, nay was, intolerable.

"James,"—she turned to him frankly— "why have you not come over to see us lately as often as you did? Charles misses you sadly, and so do I. Prepare to find him in a bad mood to-day. But just now he distressed Mr. Dorriforth by his unreasonableness touching the railroad." She smiled and went on lightly, "He said that you were a false friend to him—a traitor!"

And then Catherine Nagle stopped and caught her breath. God! Why had she said that? But Mottram had evidently not caught the sinister word, and Catherine in haste drove back conscience into the lair whence conscience had leapt so suddenly to her side.

"Maybe I ought, in this matter of the railroad," he said musingly, "to have humoured Charles. I am now sorry I did not do so. After all, Charles may be right—and all we others wrong. The railroad may not bring us lasting good!"

Catherine looked at him surprised. James Mottram had always been so sure of himself in this matter; but now there was dejection, weariness in his voice; and he was walking quickly, more quickly up the steep incline than Mrs. Nagle found agreeable. But she also hastened her steps, telling herself, with wondering pain, that he was evidently in no mood for her company.

"Mr. Dorriforth has already been here two days," she observed irrelevantly.

"Aye, I know that. It was to see him I came to-day; and I will ask you to spare him to me for two or three hours. Indeed, I propose that he should walk back with me to the Eype. I wish him to witness my new will. And then I may as well go to confession, for it is well to be shriven before a journey, though for my part I feel ever safer on sea than land!"

Mottram looked straight before him as he spoke.

"A journey?" Catherine repeated the words in a low, questioning tone. There had come across her heart a feeling of such anguish that it was as though her body instead of her soul were being wrenched asunder. In her extremity she called on pride—and pride, ever woman's most loyal friend, flew to her aid.

"Yes," he repeated, still staring straight in front of him, "I leave to-morrow for Plymouth. I have had letters from my agent in Jamaica which make it desirable that I should return there without delay." He dug his stick into the soft earth as he spoke.

James Mottram was absorbed in himself, in his own desire to carry himself well in his fierce determination to avoid betraying what he believed to be his secret. But Catherine

Nagle knew nothing of this. She almost thought him indifferent.

They had come to a steep part of the incline, and Catherine suddenly quickened her steps and passed him, so making it impossible that he could see her face. She tried to speak, but the commonplace words she desired to say were strangled, at birth, in her throat.

"Charles will not mind; he will not miss me as he would have missed me before this unhappy business of the railroad came between us," Mottram said lamely.

She still made no answer; instead she shook her head with an impatient gesture. Her silence made him sorry. After all, he had been a good friend to Catherine Nagle—so much he could tell himself without shame. He stepped aside on to the grass, and striding forward turned round and faced her.

The tears were rolling down her cheeks; but she threw back her head and met his gaze with a cold, almost a defiant look. "You startled me greatly," she said breathlessly, "and took me so by surprise, James! I am grieved to think how Charles—nay, how we shall both—miss you. It is of Charles I think, James; it is for Charles I weep——"

As she uttered the lying words, she still

looked proudly into his face as if daring him to doubt her. "But I shall never forget—I shall ever think with gratitude of your great goodness to my poor Charles. Two years out of your life—that's what it's been, James. Too much—too much by far!" She had regained control over her quivering heart, and it was with a wan smile that she added, "But we shall miss you, dear, kind friend."

Her smile stung him. "Catherine," he said sternly, "I go because I must—because I dare not stay. You are a woman and a saint, I a man and a sinner. I've been a fool and worse than a fool. You say that Charles to-day called me false friend, traitor! Catherine—Charles spoke more truly than he knew."

His burning eyes held her fascinated. The tears had dried on her cheeks. She was thirstily absorbing the words as they fell now slowly, now quickly, from his lips.

But what was this he was saying? "Catherine, do you wish me to go on?" Oh, cruel! Cruel to put this further weight on her conscience! But she made a scarcely perceptible movement of assent—and again he spoke.

"Years ago I thought I loved you. I went away, as you know well, because of that love.

You had chosen Charles—Charles in many ways the better fellow of the two. I went away thinking myself sick with love of you, but it was false—only my pride had been hurt. I did not love you as I loved myself. And when I got clear away, in a new place, among new people"—he hesitated and reddened darkly —"I forgot you! I vow that when I came back I was cured—cured if ever a man was! It was of Charles, not of you, Catherine, that I thought on my way home. To me Charles and you had become one. I swear it!" He repeated: "To me you and Charles were one."

He waited a long moment, and then, more slowly, he went on, as if pleading with himself—with her: "You know what I found here in place of what I had left? I found Charles a——"

Catherine Nagle shrank back. She put up her right hand to ward off the word, and Mottram, seizing her hand, held it in his with a convulsive clasp. "'Twas not the old feeling that came back to me—that I again swear, Catherine. 'Twas something different —something infinitely stronger—something that at first I believed to be all noble——"

He stopped speaking, and Catherine Nagle uttered one word—a curious word. "When?"

ST. CATHERINE'S EVE

she asked, and more urgently again she whispered, "When?"

"Long before I knew!" he said hoarsely. "At first I called the passion that possessed me by the false name of 'friendship.' But that poor hypocrisy soon left me! A month ago, Catherine, I found myself wishing—I'll say this for myself, it was for the first time—that Charles was dead. And then I knew for sure what I had already long suspected—that the time had come for me to go——"

He dropped her hand, and stood before her, abased in his own eyes, but one who, if a criminal, had had the strength to be his own judge and pass heavy sentence on himself.

"And now, Catherine—now that you understand why I go, you will bid me God-speed. Nay, more"—he looked at her, and smiled wryly—"if you are kind, as I know you to be kind, you will pray for me, for I go from you a melancholy, as well as a foolish man."

She smiled a strange little wavering smile, and Mottram was deeply moved by the gentleness with which Catherine Nagle had listened to his story. He had been prepared for an averted glance, for words of cold rebuke—such words as his own long-dead mother would surely have uttered to a man who had come to her with such a tale.

They walked on for a while, and Catherine again broke the silence by a question which disturbed her companion. "Then your agent's letter was not really urgent, James?"

"The letters of an honest agent always call for the owner," he muttered evasively.

They reached the orchard gate. Catherine held the key in her hand, but she did not place it in the lock—instead she paused awhile. "Then there is no special urgency?" she repeated. "And James—forgive me for asking it—are you, indeed, leaving England because of this—this matter of which you have just told me?"

He bent his head in answer.

Then she said deliberately: "Your conscience, James, is too scrupulous. I do not think that there is any reason why you should not stay. When Charles and I were in Italy," she went on in a toneless, monotonous voice, "I met some of those young noblemen who in times of pestilence go disguised to nurse the sick and bury the dead. It is that work of charity, dear friend, which you have been performing in our unhappy house. You have been nursing the sick—nay, more, you have been tending"—she waited, then in a low voice she added—"the dead—the dead that are yet alive."

Mottram's soul leapt into his eyes. "Then you bid me stay?" he asked.

"For the present," she answered, "I beg you to stay. But only so if it is indeed true that your presence is not really required in Jamaica."

"I swear, Catherine, that all goes sufficiently well there." Again he fixed his honest, ardent eyes on her face.

And now James Mottram was filled with a great exultation of spirit. He felt that Catherine's soul, incapable of even the thought of evil, shamed and made unreal the temptation which had seemed till just now one which could only be resisted by flight. Catherine was right; he had been over scrupulous.

There was proof of it in the blessed fact that even now, already, the poison which had seemed to possess him, that terrible longing for another man's wife, had left him, vanishing in that same wife's pure presence. It was when he was alone—alone in his great house on the hill, that the devil entered into him, whispering that it was an awful thing such a woman as was Catherine, sensitive, intelligent, and in her beauty so appealing, should be tied to such a being as was Charles Nagle—poor Charles, whom every one, excepting his wife and one loyal kinsman, called mad. And yet now it was for this very Charles that Catherine asked him to stay, for the sake of that unhappy, distraught man to whom he, James Mottram, recognized the duty of a brother.

"We will both forget what *you* have just told me," she said gently, and he bowed his head in reverence.

They were now on the last step of the stone stairway leading to the terrace.

Mrs. Nagle turned to her companion; he saw that her eyes were very bright, and that the rose-red colour in her cheeks had deepened as if she had been standing before a great fire.

As they came within sight of Charles Nagle and of the old priest, Catherine put out her hand. She touched Mottram on the arm—it was a fleeting touch, but it brought them both, with beating hearts, to a stand. "James," she said, and then she stopped for a moment —a moment that seemed to contain æons of mingled rapture and pain—"one word about Mr. Dorriforth." The commonplace words dropped them back to earth. "Did you wish him to stay with you till to-morrow? That will scarcely be possible, for to-morrow is St. Catherine's Day."

"Why, no," he said quickly. "I will not take him home with me to-night. All my plans are now changed. My will can wait"—he smiled at her—"and so can my confession."

"No, no!" she cried almost violently. "Your confession must not wait, James——"

"Aye, but it must," he said, and again he smiled. "I am in no mood for confession, Catherine." He added in a lower tone, "you've purged me of my sin, my dear—I feel already shriven."

Shame of a very poignant quality suddenly seared Catherine Nagle's soul. "Go on, you," she said breathlessly, though to his ears she seemed to speak in her usual controlled and quiet tones, "I have some orders to give in the house. Join Charles and Mr. Dorriforth. I will come out presently."

James Mottram obeyed her. He walked quickly forward. "Good news, Charles," he cried. "These railway men whose presence so offends you go for good to-morrow! Reverend sir, accept my hearty greeting."

Catherine Nagle turned to the right and went into the house. She hastened through the rooms in which, year in and year out, she spent her life, with Charles as her perpetual, her insistent companion. She now longed for a time of recollection and secret communion, and so she instinctively made for the one place where no one, not even Charles, would come and disturb her.

Walking across the square hall, she ran up the broad staircase leading to the gallery, out of which opened the doors of her bedroom and of her husband's dressing-room. But she went swiftly past these two closed doors, and made her way along a short passage which terminated abruptly with a faded red baize door giving access to the chapel.

Long, low-ceilinged and windowless, the chapel of Edgecombe Manor had remained unaltered since the time when there were heavy penalties attached both to the celebration of the sacred rites and to the hearing of Mass. The chapel depended for what fresh air it had on a narrow door opening straight on to ladder-like stairs leading down directly and out on to the terrace below. It was by this way that the small and scattered congregation gained access to the chapel when the presence of a priest permitted of Mass being celebrated there.

Catherine went up close to the altar rails,

and sat down on the arm-chair placed there for her sole use. She felt that now, when about to wrestle with her soul, she could not kneel and pray. Since she had been last in the chapel, acting sacristan that same morning, life had taken a great stride forward, dragging her along in its triumphant wake, a cruel and yet a magnificent conqueror.

Hiding her face in her hands, she lived again each agonized and exquisite moment she had lived through as there had fallen on her ears the words of James Mottram's shamed confession. Once more her heart was moved to an exultant sense of happiness that he should have said these things to her—of happiness and shrinking shame. . . .

But soon other thoughts, other and sterner memories were thrust upon her. She told herself the bitter truth. Not only had she led James Mottram into temptation, but she had put all her woman's wit to the task of keeping him there. It was her woman's wit—but Catherine Nagle called it by a harsher name— which had enabled her to make that perilous rock on which she and James Mottram now stood heart to heart together, appear, to him at least, a spot of sanctity and safety. It was she, not the man who had gazed at her with so ardent a belief in her purity and honour, who was playing traitor—and traitor to one at once confiding and defenceless. . . .

Then, strangely, this evocation of Charles brought her burdened conscience relief. Catherine found sudden comfort in remembering her care, her tenderness for Charles. She reminded herself fiercely that never had she allowed anything to interfere with her wifely duty. Never? Alas! she remembered that there had come a day, at a time when James Mottram's sudden defection had filled her heart with pain, when she had been unkind to Charles. She recalled his look of bewildered surprise, and how he, poor fellow, had tried to sulk—only a few hours later to come to her, as might have done a repentant child, with the words, "Have I offended you, dear love?" And she who now avoided his caresses had kissed him of her own accord with tears, and cried, "No, no, Charles, you never offend me—you are always good to me!"

There had been a moment to-day, just before she had taunted James Mottram with being over-scrupulous, when she had told herself that she could be loyal to both of these men she loved and who loved her, giving to each a different part of her heart.

But that bargain with conscience had never been struck; while considering it she had found herself longing for some convulsion of the earth which should throw her and Mottram in each other's arms.

James Mottram traitor? That was what she was about to make him be. Catherine forced herself to face the remorse, the horror, the loathing of himself which would ensue.

It was for Mottram's sake, far more than in response to the command laid on her by her own soul, that Catherine Nagle finally determined on the act of renunciation which she knew was being immediately required of her.

When Mrs. Nagle came out on the terrace the three men rose ceremoniously. She glanced at Charles, even now her first thought and her first care. His handsome face was overcast with the look of gloomy preoccupation which she had learnt to fear, though she knew that in truth it signified but little. At James Mottram she did not look, for she wished to husband her strength for what she was about to do.

Making a sign to the others to sit down, she herself remained standing behind Charles's chair. It was from there that she at last spoke, instinctively addressing her words to the old priest.

"I wonder," she said, "if James has told

you of his approaching departure? He has heard from his agent in Jamaica that his presence is urgently required there."

Charles Nagle looked up eagerly. "This is news indeed!" he exclaimed. "Lucky fellow! Why, you'll escape all the trouble that you've put on us with regard to that puffing devil!" He spoke more cordially than he had done for a long time to his cousin.

Mr. Dorriforth glanced for a moment up at Catherine's face. Then quickly he averted his eyes.

James Mottram rose to his feet. His limbs seemed to have aged. He gave Catherine a long, probing look.

"Forgive me," he said deliberately. "You mistook my meaning. The matter is not as urgent, Catherine, as you thought." He turned to Charles, "I will not desert my friends—at any rate not for the present. I'll face the puffing devil with those to whom I have helped to acquaint him!"

But Mrs. Nagle and the priest both knew that the brave words were a vain boast. Charles alone was deceived; and he showed no pleasure in the thought that the man who had been to him so kind and so patient a comrade and so trusty a friend was after all not leaving England immediately.

"I must be going back to the Eype now." Mottram spoke heavily; again he looked at Mrs. Nagle with a strangely probing, pleading look. "But I'll come over to-morrow morning—to Mass. I've not forgotten that to-morrow is St. Catherine's Day—that this is St. Catherine's Eve."

Charles seemed to wake out of a deep abstraction. "Yes, yes," he said heartily. "To-morrow is the great day! And then, after we've had breakfast I shall be able to consult you, James, about a very important matter, that new well they're plaguing me to sink in the village."

For the moment the cloud had again lifted; Nagle looked at his cousin with all his old confidence and affection, and in response James Mottram's face worked with sudden emotion.

"I'll be quite at your service, Charles," he said, "quite at your service!"

Catherine stood by. "I will let you out by the orchard gate," she said. "No need for you to go round by the road."

They walked, silently, side by side, along the terrace and down the stone steps. When in the leafless orchard, and close to where they were to part, he spoke:

"You bid me go—at once?" Mottram asked the question in a low, even tone; but he did not look at Catherine, instead his eyes seemed to be following the movements of the stick he was digging into the ground at their feet.

"I think, James, that would be best." Even to herself the words Mrs. Nagle uttered sounded very cold.

"Best for me?" he asked. Then he looked up, and with sudden passion, "Catherine!" he cried. "Believe me, I know that I can stay! Forget the wild and foolish things I said. No thought of mine shall wrong Charles —I swear it solemnly. Catherine!—do not bid me leave you. Cannot you trust my honour?" His eyes held hers, by turns they seemed to become beseeching and imperious.

Catherine Nagle suddenly threw out her hands with a piteous gesture. "Ah! James," she said, "I cannot trust my own——" And as she thus made surrender of her two most cherished possessions, her pride and her womanly reticence, Mottram's face—the plain-featured face so exquisitely dear to her—became transfigured. He said no word, he made no step forward, and yet Catherine felt as if the whole of his being was calling her, drawing her to him. . . .

Suddenly there rang through the still air a discordant cry: "Catherine! Catherine!"

Mrs. Nagle sighed, a long convulsive sigh. It was as though a deep pit had opened between herself and her companion. "That was Charles," she whispered, "poor Charles calling me. I must not keep him waiting."

"God forgive me," Mottram said huskily, "and bless you, Catherine, for all your goodness to me." He took her hand in farewell, and she felt the firm, kind grasp to be that of the kinsman and friend, not that of the lover.

Then came over her a sense of measureless and most woeful loss. She realized for the first time all that his going away would mean to her—of all that it would leave her bereft. He had been the one human being to whom she had been able to bring herself to speak freely. Charles had been their common charge, the link as well as the barrier between them.

"You'll come to-morrow morning?" she said, and she tried to withdraw her hand from his. His impersonal touch hurt her.

"I'll come to-morrow, and rather early, Catherine. Then I'll be able to confess before Mass." He was speaking in his usual voice, but he still held her hand, and she felt his grip on it tightening, bringing welcome hurt.

"And you'll leave——?"

"For Plymouth to-morrow afternoon," he said briefly. He dropped her hand, which now felt numbed and maimed, and passed through the gate without looking back.

She stood a moment watching him as he strode down the field path. It had suddenly become, from day, night,—high time for Charles to be indoors.

Forgetting to lock the gate, she turned and retraced her steps through the orchard, and so made her way up to where her husband and the old priest were standing awaiting her.

As she approached them, she became aware that something going on in the valley below was absorbing their close attention. She felt glad that this was so.

"There it is!" cried Charles Nagle angrily. "I told you that they'd begin their damned practice again to-night!"

Slowly through the stretch of open country which lay spread to their right, the Bridport Wonder went puffing its way. Lanterns had been hung in front of the engine, and as it crawled sinuously along it looked like some huge monster with myriad eyes. As it entered the wood below, the dark barrel-like body of the engine seemed to give a bound, a lurch forward, and the men that manned it laughed out suddenly and loudly. The sound of their uncouth mirth floated upwards through the twilight.

"James's ale has made them merry!" exclaimed Charles, wagging his head. "And he, going through the wood, will just have met the puffing devil. I wish him the joy of the meeting!"

II

It was five hours later. Mrs. Nagle had bidden her reverend guest good night, and she was now moving about her large, barely furnished bedchamber, waiting for her husband to come upstairs.

The hours which had followed James Mottram's departure had seemed intolerably long. Catherine felt as if she had gone through some terrible physical exertion which had left her worn out—stupefied. And yet she could not rest. Even now her day was not over; Charles often grew restless and talkative at night. He and Mr. Dorriforth were no doubt still sitting talking together downstairs.

Mrs. Nagle could hear her husband's valet moving about in the next room, and the servant's proximity disturbed her.

She waited awhile and then went and opened

the door of the dressing-room. "You need not sit up, Collins," she said.

The man looked vaguely disturbed. "I fear that Mr. Nagle, madam, has gone out of doors," he said.

Catherine felt dismayed. The winter before Charles had once stayed out nearly all night.

"Go you to bed, Collins," she said. "I will wait up till Mr. Nagle comes in, and I will make it right with him."

He looked at her doubtingly. Was it possible that Mrs. Nagle was unaware of how much worse than usual his master had been the last few days?

"I fear Mr. Nagle is not well to-day," he ventured. "He seems much disturbed to-night."

"Your master is disturbed because Mr. Mottram is again leaving England for the Indies." Catherine forced herself to say the words. She was dully surprised to see how quietly news so momentous to her was received by her faithful servant.

"That may be it," said the man consideringly, "but I can't help thinking that the master is still much concerned about the rail-road. I fear that he has gone down to the wood to-night."

Catherine was startled. "Oh, surely he would

not do that, Collins?" She added in a lower tone, "I myself locked the orchard gate."

"If that is so," he answered, obviously relieved, "then with your leave, madam, I'll be off to bed."

Mrs. Nagle went back into her room, and sat down by the fire, and then, sooner than she had expected to do so, she heard a familiar sound. It came from the chapel, for Charles was fond of using that strange and secret entry into his house.

She got up and quietly opened her bedroom door.

From the hall below was cast up the dim light of the oil-lamp which always burnt there at night, and suddenly Catherine saw her husband emerge from the chapel passage, and begin walking slowly round the opposite side of the gallery. She watched him with languid curiosity.

Charles Nagle was treading softly, his head bent as if in thought. Suddenly he stayed his steps by a half-moon table on which stood a large Chinese bowl filled with pot-pourri; and into this he plunged his hands, seeming to lave them in the dry rose-leaves. Catherine felt no surprise, she was so used to his strange ways; and more than once he had hidden things—magpie fashion—in that great bowl.

She turned and closed her door noiselessly; Charles much disliked being spied on.

At last she heard him go into his dressing-room. Then came the sounds of cupboard doors being flung open, and the hurried pouring out of water. . . . But long before he could have had time to undress, she heard the familiar knock.

She said feebly, "Come in," and the door opened.

It was as she had feared; her husband had no thought, no intention, of going yet to bed. Not only was he fully dressed, but the white evening waistcoat he had been wearing had been changed by him within the last few moments for a waistcoat she had not seen before, though she had heard of its arrival from London. It was of cashmere, the latest freak of fashion. She also saw with surprise that his nankeen trousers were stained, as if he had been kneeling on damp ground. He looked very hot, his wavy hair lay damply on his brow, and he appeared excited, oppressively alive.

"Catherine!" he exclaimed, hurrying up to the place where she was standing near the fire. "You will bear witness that I was always and most positively averse to the railroad being brought here?" He did not wait for her to answer him. "Did I not always say that trouble would come of it—trouble to us all? Yet sometimes it's an ill thing to be proved right."

"Indeed it is, Charles," she answered gently. "But let us talk of this to-morrow. It's time for bed, my dear, and I am very weary."

He was now standing by her, staring down into the fire.

Suddenly he turned and seized her left arm. He brought her unresisting across the room, then dragged aside the heavy yellow curtains which had been drawn before the central window.

"Look over there, Catherine," he said meaningly. "Can you see the Eype? The moon gives but little light to-night, but the stars are bright. I can see a glimmer at yon window. They must be still waiting for James to come home."

"I see the glimmer you mean," she said dully. "No doubt they leave a lamp burning all night, as we do. James must have got home hours ago, Charles." She saw that the cuff of her husband's coat was also covered with dark, damp stains, and again she wondered uneasily what he had been doing out of doors.

"Catherine?" Charles Nagle turned her round, ungently, and forced her to look up into his face. "Have you ever thought what 'twould be like to live at the Eype?"

The question startled her. She roused herself to refute what she felt to be an unworthy accusation. "No, Charles," she said, looking at him steadily. "God is my witness that at no time did I think of living at the Eype! Such a wish never came to me——"

"Nor to me!" he cried, "nor to me, Catherine! All the long years that James Mottram was in Jamaica the thought never once came to me that he might die, and I survive him. After all we were much of an age, he had but two years the advantage of me. I always thought that the boy—my aunt's son, curse him!—would get it all. Then, had I thought of it—and I swear I never did think of it—I should have told myself that any day James might bring a wife to the Eype——"

He was staring through the leaded panes with an intent, eager gaze. "It is a fine house, Catherine, and commodious. Larger, airier than ours—though perhaps colder," he added thoughtfully. "Cold I always found it in winter when I used to stay there as a boy—colder than this house. You prefer Edgecombe, Catherine? If you were given a choice, is it here that you would live?" He looked at her, as if impatient for an answer.

"Every stone of Edgecombe, our home, is dear to me," she said solemnly. "I have never admired the Eype. It is too large, too cold for my taste. It stands too much exposed to the wind."

"It does! it does!" There was a note of regret in his voice. He let the curtain fall and looked about him rather wildly.

"And now, Charles," she said, "shall we not say our prayers and retire to rest."

"If I had only thought of it," he said, "I might have said my prayers in the chapel. But there was much to do. I thought of calling you, Catherine, for you make a better sacristan than I. Then I remembered Boney—poor little Boney crushed by the miller's dray—and how you cried all night, and that though I promised you a far finer, cleverer dog than that poor old friend had ever been. Collins said, 'Why, sir, you should have hid the old dog's death from the mistress till the morning!' A worthy fellow, Collins. He meant no disrespect to me. At that time, d'you remember, Collins had only been in my service a few months?"

It was an hour later. From where she lay in bed, Catherine Nagle with dry, aching eyes stared into the fire, watching the wood embers turn from red to grey. By her side, his hand in hers, Charles slept the dreamless, heavy slumber of a child.

Scarcely breathing, in her anxiety lest he should wake, she loosened her hand, and with a quick movement slipped out of bed. The fire was burning low, but Catherine saw everything in the room very clearly, and she threw over her night-dress a long cloak, and wound about her head the scarf which she had worn during her walk to the wood.

It was not the first time Mrs. Nagle had risen thus in the still night and sought refuge from herself and from her thoughts in the chapel; and her husband had never missed her from his side.

As she crept round the dimly lit gallery she passed by the great bowl of pot-pourri by which Charles Nagle had lingered, and there came to her the thought that it might perchance be well for her to discover, before the servants should have a chance of doing so, what he had doubtless hidden there.

Catherine plunged both her hands into the scented rose-leaves, and she gave a sudden cry of pain—for her fingers had closed on the sharp edge of a steel blade. Then she drew out a narrow damascened knife, one which her husband, taken by its elegant shape, had purchased long before in Italy.

Mrs. Nagle's brow furrowed in vexation—Collins should have put the dangerous toy out of his master's reach. Slipping the knife into the deep pocket of her cloak, she hurried on into the unlit passage leading to the chapel.

Save for the hanging lamp, which since Mr. Dorriforth had said Mass there that morning signified the presence of the Blessed Sacrament, the chapel should have been in darkness. But as Catherine passed through the door she saw, with sudden, uneasy amazement, the farther end of the chapel in a haze of brightness.

Below the altar, striking upwards from the floor of the sanctuary, gleamed a corona of light. Charles—she could not for a moment doubt that it was Charles's doing—had moved the six high, heavy silver candlesticks which always stood on either side of the altar, and had placed them on the ground.

There, in a circle, the wax candles blazed, standing sentinel-wise about a dark, round object which was propped up on a pile of altar-linen carefully arranged to support it.

Fear clutched at Catherine's heart—such fear as even in the early days of Charles's madness had never clutched it. She was filled with a horrible dread, and a wild, incredulous dismay.

What was the Thing, at once so familiar and so terribly strange, that Charles had brought out of the November night and placed with so much care below the altar?

But the thin flames of the candles, now shooting up, now guttering low, blown on by some invisible current of strong air, gave no steady light.

Staying still close to the door, she sank down on her knees, and desiring to shut out, obliterate, the awful sight confronting her, she pressed both her hands to her eyes. But that availed her nothing.

Suddenly there rose up before Catherine Nagle a dreadful scene of that great Revolution drama of which she had been so often told as a child. She saw, with terrible distinctness, the severed heads of men and women borne high on iron pikes, and one of these blood-streaked, livid faces was that of James Mottram—the wide-open, sightless eyes, his eyes. . . .

There also came back to her as she knelt there, shivering with cold and anguish, the story of a French girl of noble birth who, having bought her lover's head from the executioner, had walked with it in her arms to the village near Paris where stood his deserted château.

Slowly she rose from her knees, and with her hands thrown out before her, she groped her way to the wall and there crept along, as if a precipice lay on her other side.

At last she came to the narrow oak door which gave on to the staircase leading into the open air. The door was ajar; it was from there that blew the current of air which caused those thin, fantastic flames to flare and gutter in the awful stillness.

She drew the door to, and went on her way, so round to the altar. In the now steadier light Catherine saw that the large missal lay open at the Office for the Dead.

She laid her hands with a blind instinct upon the altar, and felt a healing touch upon their palms. Henceforth—and Catherine Nagle was fated to live many long years—she remained persuaded that it was then there had come to her a shaft of divine light piercing the dark recesses of her soul. For it was at that moment that there came to her the conviction, and one which never faltered, that Charles Nagle had done no injury to James Mottram. And there also came to her then the swift understanding of what others would believe, were there to be found in the private chapel of Edgecombe

Manor that which now lay on the ground behind her, close to her feet.

So understanding, Catherine suddenly saw the way open before her, and the dread thing which she must do if Charles were to be saved from a terrible suspicion—one which would undoubtedly lead to his being taken away from her and from all that his poor, atrophied heart held dear, to be asylumed.

With steps that did not falter, Catherine Nagle went behind the altar into the little sacristy, there to seek in the darkness an altar-cloth.

Holding the cloth up before her face she went back into the lighted chapel, and kneeling down, she uncovered her face and threw the cloth over what lay before her.

And then Catherine's teeth began to chatter, and a mortal chill overtook her. She was being faced by a new and to her a most dread enemy, for till to-night she and that base physical fear which is the coward's foe had never met. Pressing her hands together, she whispered the short, simple prayer for the Faithful Departed that she had said so often and, she now felt, so unmeaningly. Even as she uttered the familiar words, base Fear slunk away, leaving in his place her soul's old companion, Courage, and his attendant, Peace.

She rose to her feet, and opening wide her eyes forced herself to think out what must be done by her in order that no trace of Charles's handiwork should remain in the chapel.

Snuffing out the wicks, Catherine lifted the candlesticks from the ground and put them back in their accustomed place upon the altar. Then, stooping, she forced herself to wrap up closely in the altar-cloth that which must be her burden till she found James Mottram's headless body where Charles had left it, and placing that same precious burden within the ample folds of her cloak, she held it with her left hand and arm closely pressed to her bosom. . . .

With her right hand she gathered up the pile of stained altar-linen from the ground, and going once more into the sacristy she thrust it into the oak chest in which were kept the Lenten furnishings of the altar. Having done that, and walking slowly lest she should trip and fall, she made her way to the narrow door Charles had left open to the air, and going down the steep stairway was soon out of doors in the dark and windy night.

Charles had been right, the moon gave but little light; enough, however, so she told herself, for the accomplishment of her task.

She sped swiftly along the terrace, keeping

close under the house, and then more slowly walked down the stone steps where last time she trod them Mottram had been her companion, his living lips as silent as were his dead lips now.

The orchard gate was wide open, and as she passed through there came to Catherine Nagle the knowledge why Charles on his way back from the wood had not even latched it; he also, when passing through it, had been bearing a burden. . . .

She walked down the field path; and when she came to the steep place where Mottram had told her that he was going away, the tears for the first time began running down Catherine's face. She felt again the sharp, poignant pain which his then cold and measured words had dealt her, and the blow this time fell on a bruised heart. With a convulsive gesture she pressed more closely that which she was holding to her desolate breast.

At night the woodland is strangely, curiously alive. Catherine shuddered as she heard the stuffless sounds, the tiny rustlings and burrowings of those wild, shy creatures whose solitude had lately been so rudely invaded, and who now of man's night made their day. Their myriad presence made her human loneliness more intense than it had been in the open fields, and as she started walking by the side of the iron rails, her eyes fixed on the dark drift of dead leaves which dimly marked the path, she felt solitary indeed, and beset with vague and fearsome terrors.

At last she found herself nearing the end of the wood. Soon would come the place where what remained of the cart-track struck sharply to the left, up the hill towards the Eype.

It was there, close to the open, that Catherine Nagle's quest ended; and that she was able to accomplish the task she had set herself, of making that which Charles had rendered incomplete, complete as men, considering the flesh, count completeness.

Within but a few yards of safety, James Mottram had met with death; a swift, merciful death, due to the negligence of an engine-driver not only new to his work but made blindly merry by Mottram's gift of ale.

Charles Nagle woke late on the morning of St. Catherine's Day, and the pale November sun fell on the fully dressed figures of his wife and Mr. Dorriforth standing by his bedside.

But Charles, absorbed as always in himself, saw nothing untoward in their presence.

"I had a dream!" he exclaimed. "A most horrible and gory dream this night! I thought I was in the wood; James Mottram lay before me, done to death by that puffing devil we saw slithering by so fast. His head nearly severed—*à la guillotine,* you understand, my love?—from his poor body——"

There was a curious, secretive smile on Charles Nagle's pale, handsome face.

Catherine Nagle gave a cry, a stifled shriek of horror.

The priest caught her by the arm and led her to the couch which stood across the end of the bed.

"Charles," he said sternly, "this is no light matter. Your dream—there's not a doubt of it—was sent you in merciful preparation for the awful truth. Your kinsman, your almost brother, Charles, was found this morning in the wood, dead as you saw him in your dream."

The face of the man sitting up in bed stiffened—was it with fear or grief? "They found James Mottram dead?" he repeated with an uneasy glance in the direction of the couch where crouched his wife. "And his head, most reverend sir—what of his head?"

"James Mottram's body was terribly mangled. But his head," answered the priest solemnly, "was severed from his body, as you saw it in your dream, Charles. A strangely clean cut, it seems——"

"Ay," said Charles Nagle. "That was in my dream too; if I said nearly severed, I said wrong."

Catherine was now again standing by the priest's side.

"Charles," she said gravely, "you must now get up; Mr. Dorriforth is only waiting for you, to say Mass for James's soul."

She made the sign of the cross, and then, with her right hand shading her sunken eyes, she went on, "My dear, I entreat you to tell no one—not even faithful Collins—of this awful dream. We want no such tale spread about the place——"

She looked at the old priest entreatingly, and he at once responded. "Catherine is right, Charles. We of the Faith should be more careful with regard to such matters than are the ignorant and superstitious."

But he was surprised to hear the woman by his side say insistently, "Charles, if only to please me, vow that you will keep most secret this dreadful dream. I fear that if it should come to your Aunt Felwake's ears——"

"That I swear it shall not," said Charles sullenly.

And he kept his word.

THE WOMAN FROM PURGATORY

THE WOMAN FROM PURGATORY

"... not dead, this friend—not dead,
But, in the path we mortals tread,
Got some few, little steps ahead
  And nearer to the end,
So that you, too, once past the bend,
Shall meet again, as face to face, this friend
  You fancy dead."

I

MRS. BARLOW, the prettiest and the happiest and the best dressed of the young wives of Summerfield, was walking toward the Catholic Church. She was going to consult the old priest as to her duty to an unsatisfactory servant; for Agnes Barlow was a conscientious as well as a pretty and a happy woman.

Foolish people are fond of quoting a foolish gibe: "Be good, and you may be happy; but you will not have a good time." The wise, however, soon become aware that if, in the course of life's journey, you achieve goodness and happiness, you will almost certainly have a good time too.

So, at least, Agnes Barlow had found in her own short life. Her excellent parents had built one of the first new houses in what had then been the pretty, old-fashioned village of Summerfield, some fifteen miles from London. There she had been born; there she had spent delightful years at the big convent school over the hill; there she had grown up into a singularly pretty girl; and there, finally—it had seemed quite final to Agnes—she had met the clever, fascinating young lawyer, Frank Barlow.

Frank had soon become the lover all her girl friends had envied her, and then the husband who was still—so he was fond of saying and of proving in a dozen dear little daily ways—as much in love with her as on the day they were married. They lived in a charming house called The Haven, and they were the proud parents of a fine little boy, named Francis after his father, who never had any of the tiresome ailments which afflict other people's children.

But strange, dreadful things do happen—not often, of course, but just now and again—even in this delightful world! So thought Agnes Barlow on this pleasant May afternoon; for, as she walked to church, this pretty, happy, good woman found her thoughts dwelling uncomfortably on another woman, her sometime intimate friend and contemporary, who was neither good nor happy.

This was Teresa Maldo, the lovely half-Spanish girl who had been her favourite schoolmate at the convent over the hill.

Poor, foolish, unhappy, wicked Teresa! Only ten days ago Teresa had done a thing so extraordinary, so awful, so unprecedented, that Agnes Barlow had thought of little else ever since. Teresa Maldo had eloped, gone right away from her home and her husband, and with a married man!

Teresa and Agnes were the same age; they had had the same upbringing; they were both —in a very different way, however—beautiful, and they had each been married, six years before, on the same day of the month.

But how different had been their subsequent fates!

Teresa had at once discovered that her husband drank. But she loved him, and for a while it seemed as if marriage would reform Maldo. Unfortunately, this better state of things did not last: he again began to drink: and the matrons of Summerfield soon had reason to shake their heads over the way Teresa Maldo went on.

Men, you see, were so sorry for this lovely young woman, blessed (or cursed) with what old-fashioned folk call "the come-hither eye," that they made it their business to console her for such a worthless husband as was Maldo. No wonder Teresa and Agnes drifted apart; no wonder Frank Barlow soon forbade his spotless Agnes to accept Mrs. Maldo's invitations. And Agnes knew that her dear Frank was right; she had never much enjoyed her visits to Teresa's house.

But an odd thing had happened about a fortnight ago. And it was to this odd happening that Agnes's mind persistently recurred each time she found herself alone.

About three days before Teresa Maldo had done the mad and wicked thing of which all Summerfield was still talking, she had paid a long call on Agnes Barlow.

The unwelcome guest had stayed a very long time; she had talked, as she generally did talk now, wildly and rather strangely; and Agnes, looking back, was glad to remember that no one else had come in while her old schoolfellow was there.

When, at last, Teresa Maldo had made up her mind to go (luckily, some minutes before Frank was due home from town), Agnes accompanied her to the gate of The Haven, and there the other had turned round and made such odd remarks.

"I came to tell you something!" she had exclaimed. "But, now that I see you looking so happy, so pretty, and—forgive me for saying so, Agnes—so horribly good, I feel that I can't tell you! But, Agnes, whatever happens, you must pity, and—and, if you can, understand me."

It was now painfully clear to Agnes Barlow that Teresa had come that day intending to tell her once devoted friend of the wicked thing she meant to do; and more than once pretty and good Mrs. Barlow had asked herself uneasily whether she could have done anything to stop Teresa on her downward course.

But no; Agnes felt her conscience clear. How would it have been possible for her even to discuss with Teresa so shameful a possibility as that of a woman leaving her husband with another man?

Agnes thought of the two sinners with a touch of fascinated curiosity. They were said to be in Paris, and Teresa was probably having a very good time—a wildly amusing, exciting time.

She even told herself, did this pretty, happy, fortunate young married woman, that it was strange, and not very fair, that vice and pleasure should always go together! It was just a little irritating to know that Teresa would never again be troubled by the kind of worries that played quite an important part in Agnes's own blameless life. Never again, for instance, would Teresa's cook give her notice, as Agnes's cook had given her notice that morning. It was about that matter she wished to see Father Ferguson, for it was through the priest she had heard of the impertinent Irish girl who cooked so well, but who had such an independent manner, and who would *not* wear a cap!

Yes, it certainly seemed unfair that Teresa would now be rid of all domestic worries—nay, more, that the woman who had sinned would live in luxurious hotels, motoring and shopping all day, going to the theatre or to a music-hall each night.

At last, however, Agnes dismissed Teresa Maldo from her mind. She knew that it is not healthy to dwell overmuch on such people and their doings.

The few acquaintances Mrs. Barlow met on her way smiled and nodded, but, as she was walking rather quickly, no one tried to stop her. She had chosen the back way to the church because it was the prettiest way, and also because it would take her by a house where a friend of hers was living in lodgings.

And suddenly the very friend in question—his name was Ferrier—came out of his lodgings. He had a tall, slight, active figure; he was dressed in a blue serge suit, and, though it was still early spring, he wore a straw hat.

Agnes smiled a little inward smile. She was, as we already know, a very good as well as a happy woman. But a woman as pretty as was Agnes Barlow meets with frequent pleasant occasions of withstanding temptation, of which those about her, especially her dear parents and her kind husband, are often curiously unknowing. And the tall, well-set-up masculine figure now hurrying toward her with such eager steps played a considerable part in Agnes's life, if only as constantly providing her with occasions of acquiring merit.

Agnes knew very well—even the least imaginative woman is always acutely conscious of such a fact—that, had she not been a prudent and a ladylike as well as (of course) a very good woman, this clever, agreeable, interesting young man would have made love to her. As it was, he (of course) did nothing of the kind. He did not even try to flirt with her, as our innocent Agnes understood that much-tried verb; and she regarded their friendship as a pleasant interlude in her placid, well-regulated existence, and as a most excellent influence on his more agitated life.

Mr. Ferrier lifted his hat. He smiled down into Agnes's blue eyes. What very charming, nay, what beautiful eyes they were! Deeply, exquisitely blue, but unshadowed, as innocent of guile, as are a child's eyes.

"Somehow, I had a kind of feeling that you would be coming by just now," he said in a rather hesitating voice; "so I left my work and came out on chance."

Now, Agnes was very much interested in Mr. Ferrier's work. Mr. Ferrier was not only a writer—the only writer she had ever known; he was also a poet. She had been pleasantly thrilled the day he had given her a slim little book, on each page of which was a poem. This gift had been made when they had known each other only two months, and he had inscribed it: "From G. G. F. to A. M. B."

Mr. Ferrier had a charming studio flat in Chelsea, that odd, remote place where London artists live, far from the pleasant London of the shops and theatres which was all Agnes knew of the great City near which she dwelt. But he always spent the summer in the country, and his summer lasted from the 1st of May till the 1st of October. He had already spent two holidays at Summerfield, and had been a great deal at The Haven.

When with Mr. Ferrier, and they were much together during the long week-days when Summerfield is an Adamless Eden, Agnes Barlow made a point of often speaking of dear Frank and of Frank's love for her,—not, of course, in a way that any one could have regarded as silly, but in a natural, happy, simple way.

How easy, how very easy, it is to keep this kind of friendship—friendship between a man and a woman—within bounds! And how terribly sad it was to think that Teresa Maldo had not known how to do that easy thing! But then, Teresa's lover had been a married man separated from his wife, and that doubtless made all the difference. Agnes Barlow could assure herself in all sincerity that, had Mr. Ferrier been the husband of another woman, she would never have allowed him to become her friend to the extent that he was now.

Mr. Ferrier—Agnes never allowed herself to think of him as Gerald (although he had once asked her to call him by his Christian name)—held an evening paper in his hand.

"I was really on my way to The Haven," he observed, "for there are a few verses of mine in this paper which I am anxious you should read. Shall I go on and leave it at your house, or will you take it now? And then, if I may, I will call for it some time to-morrow. Should I be likely to find you in about four o'clock?"

"Yes, I'll be in about four, and I think I'll take the paper now."

And then—for she was walking very slowly, and Ferrier, with his hands behind his back, kept pace with her—Agnes could not resist the pleasure of looking down at the open sheet, for the newspaper was so turned about that she could see the little set of verses quite plainly.

The poem was called "My Lady of the Snow," and it told in very pretty, complicated language of a beautiful, pure woman whom the writer loved in a desperate but quite respectful way.

She grew rather red. "I must hurry on, for I am going to church," she said a little stiffly. "Good evening, Mr. Ferrier. Yes, I will keep the paper till to-morrow, if I may. I should like to show it to Frank. He hasn't been to the office to-day, for he isn't very well, and he will like to see an evening paper."

Mr. Ferrier lifted his hat with a rather sad look, and turned back toward the house where he lodged. And as Agnes walked on she felt disturbed and a little uncomfortable. Her clever friend had evidently been grieved by her apparent lack of appreciation of his poem.

When she reached the church her parents had helped to build, she went in, knelt down, and said a prayer. Then she got up and walked through into the sacristy. Father Ferguson was almost certain to be there just now.

Agnes Barlow had known the old priest all her life. He had baptized her; he had been chaplain at the convent during the years she had been at school there; and now he had come back to be parish priest at Summerfield.

When with Father Ferguson, Agnes somehow never felt quite so good as she did when she was by herself or with a strange priest; and yet Father Ferguson was always very kind to her.

As she came into the sacristy he looked round with a smile. "Well?" he said. "Well, Agnes, my child, what can I do for you?"

Agnes put the newspaper she was holding down on a chair. And then, to her surprise, Father Ferguson took up the paper and glanced over the front page. He was an intelligent man, and sometimes he found Summerfield a rather shut-in, stifling sort of place.

But the priest's instinctive wish to know

something of what was passing in the great world outside the suburb where it was his duty to dwell did him an ill turn, for something he read in the paper caused him to utter a low, quick exclamation of intense pain and horror.

"What's the matter?" cried Agnes Barlow, frightened out of her usual self-complacency. "Whatever has happened, Father Ferguson?"

He pointed with shaking finger to a small paragraph. It was headed "Suicide of a Lady at Dover," and Agnes read the few lines with bewildered and shocked amazement.

Teresa Maldo, whom she had visioned, only a few minutes ago, as leading a merry, gloriously careless life with her lover, was dead. She had thrown herself out of a bedroom window in a hotel at Dover, and she had been killed instantly, dashed into a shapeless mass on the stones below.

Agnes stared down at the curt, cold little paragraph with excited horror. She was six-and-twenty, but she had never seen death, and, as far as she knew, the girls with whom she had been at school were all living. Teresa—poor unhappy, sinful Teresa—had been the first to die, and by her own hand.

The old priest's eyes slowly brimmed over with tears. "Poor, unhappy child!" he said, with a break in his voice. "Poor, unfortunate

Teresa! I did not think, I should never have believed, that she would seek—and find—this terrible way out."

Agnes was a little shocked at his broken words. True, Teresa had been very unhappy, and it was right to pity her; but she had also been very wicked; and now she had put, as it were, the seal on her wickedness by killing herself.

"Three or four days before she went away she came and saw me," the priest went on, in a low, pained voice. "I did everything in my power to stop her, but I could do nothing—she had given her word!"

"Given her word?" repeated Agnes wonderingly.

"Yes," said Father Ferguson; "she had given that wretched, that wickedly selfish man her promise. She believed that if she broke her word he would kill himself. I begged her to go and see some woman—some kind, pitiful, understanding woman—but I suppose she feared lest such a one would dissuade her to more purpose than I was able to do."

Agnes looked at him with troubled eyes.

"She was very dear to my heart," the priest went on. "She was always a generous, unselfish child, and she was very, very fond of you, Agnes."

Agnes's throat tightened. What Father Ferguson said was only too true. Teresa had always been a very generous and unselfish girl, and very, very fond of her. She wondered remorsefully if she had omitted to do or say anything she could have done or said on the day that poor Teresa had come and spoken such strange, wild words——?

"It seems so awful," she said in a low voice, "so very, very awful to think that we may not even pray for her soul, Father Ferguson."

"Not pray for her soul?" the priest repeated. "Why should we not pray for the poor child's soul? I shall certainly pray for Teresa's soul every day till I die."

"But—but how can you do that, when she killed herself?"

He looked at her surprised. "And do you really so far doubt God's mercy? Surely we may hope—nay, trust—that Teresa had time to make an act of contrition?" And then he muttered something—it sounded like a line or two of poetry—which Agnes did not quite catch; but she felt, as she often did feel when with Father Ferguson, at once rebuked and rebellious.

Of course there *might* have been time for Teresa to make an act of contrition. But every one knows that to take one's life is a deadly sin. Agnes felt quite sure that if it ever occurred to herself to do such a thing she would go straight to hell. Still, she was used to obey this old priest, and that even when she did not agree with him. So she followed him into the church, and side by side they knelt down and each said a separate prayer for the soul of Teresa Maldo.

As Agnes Barlow walked slowly and soberly home, this time by the high road, she tried to remember the words, the lines of poetry, that Father Ferguson had muttered. They at once haunted and eluded her memory. Surely they could not be

> Between the window and the ground,
> She mercy sought and mercy found.

No, Agnes was sure that he had not said "window," and yet window seemed the only word that would fit the case. And he had not said, "*she* mercy found"; he had said, "*he* mercy sought and mercy found"—of that Agnes felt sure, and that, too, was odd. But then, Father Ferguson was very odd sometimes, and he was fond of quoting in his sermons queer little bits of verse of which no one had ever heard.

Suddenly she bethought herself, with more annoyance than the matter was worth, that in her agitation she had left Mr. Ferrier's newspaper in the sacristy. She did not like the thought that Father Ferguson would probably read those pretty, curious verses, "My Lady of the Snow."

Also, Agnes had actually forgotten to speak to the old priest of her impertinent cook!

II

We find Agnes Barlow again walking in Summerfield; but this time she is hurrying along the straight, unlovely cinder-strewn path which forms a short cut from the back of The Haven to Summerfield station; and the still, heavy calm of a late November afternoon broods over the rough ground on either side of her.

It is nearly six months since Teresa Maldo's elopement and subsequent suicide, and now no one ever speaks of poor Teresa, no one seems to remember that she ever lived, excepting, perhaps, Father Ferguson. . . .

As for Agnes herself, life had crowded far too many happenings into the last few weeks for her to give more than a passing thought to Teresa; indeed, the image of her dead friend rose before her only when she was saying her prayers. And as Agnes, strange to say, had grown rather careless as to her prayers, the memory of Teresa Maldo was now very faint indeed.

An awful, and to her an incredible, thing had happened to Agnes Barlow. The roof of her snug and happy House of Life had fallen in, and she lay, blinded and maimed, beneath the fragments which had been hurled down on her in one terrible moment.

Yes, it had all happened in a moment—so she now reminded herself, with the dull ache which never left her.

It was just after she had come back from Westgate with little Francis. The child had been ailing for the first time in his life, and she had taken him to the seaside for six weeks.

There, in a day, it had turned from summer to winter, raining as it only rains at the seaside; and suddenly Agnes had made up her mind to go back to her own nice, comfortable home a whole week before Frank expected her back.

Agnes sometimes acted like that—on a quick impulse; she did so to her own undoing on that dull, rainy day.

When she reached Summerfield, it was to find her telegram to her husband lying unopened on the hall table of The Haven.

Frank, it seemed, had slept in town the night before. Not that that mattered, so she told herself gleefully, full of the pleasant joy of being again in her own home; the surprise would be the greater and the more welcome when Frank did come back.

Having nothing better to do that first afternoon, Agnes had gone up to her husband's dressing-room in order to look over his summer clothes before sending them to the cleaner. In her careful, playing-at-housewifely fashion, she had turned out the pockets of his cricketing coat. There, a little to her surprise, she had found three letters, and idle curiosity as to Frank's invitations during her long stay away —Frank was deservedly popular with the ladies of Summerfield and, indeed, with all women—caused her to take the three letters out of their envelopes.

In a moment—how terrible that it should take but a moment to shatter the fabric of a human being's innocent House of Life!— Agnes had seen what had happened to her —to him. For each of these letters, written in the same sloping woman's hand, was a love letter signed "Janey"; and in each the writer, in a plaintive, delicate, but insistent and reproachful way, asked Frank for money.

Even now, though nearly seven weeks had

gone by since then, Agnes could recall with painful vividness the sick, cold feeling that had come over her—a feeling of fear rather than anger, of fear and desperate humiliation.

Locking the door of the dressing-room, she had searched eagerly—a dishonourable thing to do, as she knew well. And soon she had found other letters—letters and bills; bills of meals at restaurants, showing that her husband and a companion had constantly dined and supped at the Savoy, the Carlton, and Prince's. To those restaurants where he had taken her, Agnes, two or three times a year, laughing and grumbling at the expense, he had taken this—this *person* again and again in the short time his wife had been away.

As to the further letters, all they proved was that Frank had first met " Janey Cartwright " over some law business of hers, connected— even Agnes saw the irony of it—in some shameful way with another man; for, tied together, were a few notes signed with the writer's full name, of which the first began:

Dear Mr. Barlow:
    Forgive me for writing to your private address [etc., etc.].

The ten days that followed her discovery had seared Agnes's soul. Frank had been so dreadfully affectionate. He had pretended—she felt sure it was all pretence—to be so glad to see her again, though sometimes she caught him looking at her with cowed, miserable eyes.

More than once he had asked her solicitously if she felt ill, and she had said yes, she did feel ill, and the time at the seaside had not done her any good.

And then, on the last of those terrible ten days, Gerald Ferrier had come down to Summerfield, and both she and Frank had pressed him to stay on to dinner. He had done so, though aware that something was wrong, and he had been extraordinarily kind, sympathetic, unquestioning. But as he was leaving he had said a word to his host: "I feel worried about Mrs. Barlow"—Agnes had heard him through the window. "She doesn't look the thing, somehow! How would it be if I asked her to go with me to a private view? It might cheer her up, and perhaps she would lunch with me afterwards?" Frank had eagerly assented.

Since then Agnes had gone up to London, if not every day, very nearly every day, and Mr. Ferrier had done his best, without much success, to "cheer her up."

Though they soon became more intimate than they had ever been, Agnes never told Ferrier what it was that had turned her from a happy, unquestioning child into a miserable woman; but, of course, he guessed.

And gradually Frank also had come to know that she knew, and, man-like, he spent less and less time in his now uncomfortable home. He would go away in the morning an hour earlier than usual, and then, under pretext of business keeping him late at the office, he would come back after having dined, doubtless with "Janey," in town.

Soon Agnes began to draw a terrible comparison between these two men—between the husband who had all she had of heart, and the friend whom she now acknowledged to herself —for hypocrisy had fallen away from her—had lived only for her, and for the hours they were able to spend together, during two long years, and yet who had never told her of his love, or tried to disturb her trust in Frank.

Yes, Gerald Ferrier was all that was noble— Frank Barlow all that was ignoble. So she told herself with trembling lip a dozen times a day, taking fierce comfort in the knowledge that Ferrier was noble. But she was destined even to lose that comfort; for one day, a week before the day when we find her walking to Summerfield station, Ferrier's nobility, or what poor Agnes took to be such, suddenly broke down.

210 STUDIES IN LOVE AND IN TERROR

They had been walking together in Battersea Park, and, after one of those long silences which bespeak true intimacy between a man and a woman, he had asked her if she would come back to his rooms—for tea.

She had shaken her head smilingly. And then he had turned on her with a torrent of impetuous, burning words—words of ardent love, of anguished longing, of eager pleading. And Agnes had been frightened, fascinated, allured.

And that had not been all.

More quietly he had gone on to speak as if the code of morality in which his friend had been bred, and which had hitherto so entirely satisfied her, was, after all, nothing but a narrow counsel of perfection, suited to those who were sheltered and happy, but wretchedly inadequate to meet the needs of the greater number of human beings who are, as Agnes now was, humiliated and miserable. His words had found an echo in her sore heart, but she had not let him see how much they moved her. On the contrary, she had rebuked him, and for the first time they had quarrelled.

"If you ever speak to me like that again," she had said coldly, "I will not come again."

And once more he had turned on her

violently. "I think you had better not come again! I am but a man after all!"

They parted enemies; but the same night Ferrier wrote Agnes a very piteous letter asking pardon on his knees for having spoken as he had done. And his letter moved her to the heart. Her own deep misery—never for one moment did she forget Frank, and Frank's treachery—made her understand the torment that Ferrier was going through.

For the first time she realized, what so few of her kind ever realize, that it is a mean thing to take everything and give nothing in exchange. And gradually, as her long, solitary hours wore themselves away, Agnes came to believe that if she did what she now knew Ferrier desired her to do,—if, casting the past behind her, she started a new life with him—she would not only be doing a generous thing by the man who had loved her silently and faithfully for so long, but she would also be punishing Frank—hurting him in his honour, as he had hurt her in hers.

And then the stars that fight in their courses for those lovers who are also poets fought for Ferrier.

The day after they had quarrelled and he had written her his piteous letter of remorse, Gerald Ferrier fell ill. But he was not too ill to write. And after he had been ill four days, and when Agnes was feeling very, very miserable, he wrote and told her of a wonderful vision which had been vouchsafed to him.

In this vision Ferrier had seen Agnes knocking at the narrow front door of the lonely flat where he lived solitary; and through the door had slipped in his angelic visitant, by her mere presence bringing him peace, health, and the happiness he was schooling himself to believe must never come to him through her.

The post which brought her the letter in which Ferrier told his vision brought also to Agnes Barlow a little registered parcel containing a pearl-and-diamond pendant from Frank.

For a few moments the two lay on her knee. Then she took up the jewel and looked at it curiously. Was it with such a thing as this that her husband thought to purchase her forgiveness?

If Ferrier's letter had never been written, if Frank's gift had never been despatched, it may be doubted whether Agnes would have done what we now find her doing—hastening, that is, on her way to make Ferrier's dream come true.

At last she reached the little suburban station of Summerfield.

One of her father's many kindnesses to her each year was the gift of a season ticket to town; but to-day some queer instinct made her buy a ticket at the booking-office instead.

The booking-clerk peered out at her, surprised; then made up his mind that pretty Mrs. Barlow—she wore to-day a curiously thick veil—had a friend with her. But his long, ruminating stare made her shrink and flush. Was it possible that what she was about to do was written on her face?

She was glad indeed when the train steamed into the station. She got into an empty carriage, for the rush that goes on each evening Londonward from the suburbs had not yet begun.

And then, to her surprise, she found that it was the thought of her husband, not of the man to whom she was going to give herself, that filled her sad, embittered heart.

Old memories—memories connected with Frank, his love for her, her love for him—became insistent. She lived again, while tears forced themselves into her closed eyes, through the culminating moment of her marriage day, the start for the honeymoon,—a start made amid a crowd of laughing, cheering friends, from the little station she had just left.

She remembered the delicious tremor which

had come over her when she had found herself at last alone, really alone, with her three-hour-old bridegroom.

How infinitely kind and tender Frank had been to her!

And then Agnes reminded herself, with tightening breath, that men like Frank Barlow are always kind—too kind—to women.

Other journeys she and Frank had taken together came and mocked her, and especially the journey which had followed a month after little Francis's birth.

Frank had driven with her, the nurse, and the baby, to the station—but only to see them off. He had had a very important case in the Courts just then, and it was out of the question that he should go with his wife to Littlehampton for the change of air, the few weeks by the sea, that had been ordered by her good, careful doctor.

And then at the last moment Frank had suddenly jumped into the railway carriage without a ticket, and had gone along with her part of the way! She remembered the surprise of the monthly nurse, the woman's prim remark, when he had at last got out at Horsham, that Mr. Barlow was certainly the kindest husband she, the nurse, had ever seen.

But these memories, now so desecrated, did not make her give up her purpose. Far from it, for in a queer way they made her think more tenderly of Gerald Ferrier, whose life had been so lonely, and who had known nothing of the simpler human sanctities and joys, and who had never—so he had told her with a kind of bitter scorn of himself—been loved by any woman whom he himself could love.

In her ears there sounded Ferrier's quick, hoarsely uttered words: "D'you think I should ever have said a word to you of all this—if you had gone on being happy? D'you think I'd ask you to come to me if I thought you had any chance of being happy with him—now?"

And she knew in her soul that he had spoken truly. Ferrier would never have tried to disturb her happiness with Frank; he had never so tried during those two years when they had seen so much of each other, and when Agnes had known, deep down in her heart, that he loved her, though it had suited her conscience to pretend that his love was only "friendship."

III

The train glided into the fog-laden London station, and very slowly Agnes Barlow stepped down out of the railway carriage. She felt oppressed by the fact that she was alone. During the last few weeks Ferrier had always been standing on the platform waiting to greet her, eager to hurry her into a cab—to a picture gallery, to a concert, or of late, oftenest of all, to one of those green oases which the great town still leaves her lovers.

But now Ferrier was not here. Ferrier was ill, solitary, in the lonely rooms which he called "home."

Agnes Barlow hurried out of the station.

Hammer, hammer, hammer went what she supposed was her heart. It was a curious, to Agnes a new sensation, bred of the fear that she would meet some acquaintance to whom she would have to explain her presence in town. She could not help being glad that the fog was of that dense, stifling quality which makes every one intent on his own business rather than on that of his neighbours.

Then something happened which scared Agnes. She was walking, now very slowly, out of the station, when a tall man came up to her. He took off his hat and peered insolently into her face.

"I think I've had the pleasure of meeting you before," he said.

She stared at him with a great, unreasonable fear gripping her heart. No doubt this was some business acquaintance of Frank's. "I—I don't think so," she faltered.

"Oh, yes," he said. "Don't you remember, two years ago at the Pirola in Regent Street? I don't *think* I can be wrong."

And then Agnes understood. "You are making a mistake," she said breathlessly, and quickened her steps.

The man looked after her with a jeering smile, but he made no further attempt to molest her.

She was trembling—shaken with fear, disgust, and terror. It was odd, but such a thing had never happened to pretty Agnes Barlow before. She was not often alone in London; she had never been there alone on such a foggy evening, an evening which invited such approaches as those she had just repulsed.

She touched a respectable-looking woman on the arm. "Can you tell me the way to Flood Street, Chelsea?" she asked, her voice faltering.

"Why, yes, Miss. It's a good step from

here, but you can't mistake it. You've only got to go straight along, and then ask again after you've been walking about twenty minutes. You can't mistake it." And she hurried on, while Agnes tried to keep in step behind her, for the slight adventure outside the station became retrospectively terrifying. She thrilled with angry fear lest that—that brute should still be stalking her; but when she looked over her shoulder she saw that the pavement was nearly bare of walkers.

At last the broad thoroughfare narrowed to a point where four streets converged. Agnes glanced fearfully this way and that. Which of those shadowy black-coated figures hurrying past, intent on their business, would direct her rightly? Within the last half-hour Agnes had grown horribly afraid of men.

And then, with more relief than the fact warranted, across the narrow roadway she saw emerge, between two parting waves of fog, the shrouded figure of a woman leaning against a dead wall.

Agnes crossed the street, but as she stepped up on to the kerb, suddenly there broke from her, twice repeated, a low, involuntary cry of dread.

"Teresa!" she cried. And then, again, "Teresa!" For in the shrouded figure before her she had recognized, with a thrill of incredulous terror, the form and lineaments of Teresa Maldo.

But there came no answering cry; and Agnes gave a long, gasping, involuntary sigh of relief as she realized that what had seemed to be her dead friend's dark, glowing face was the face of a little child—a black-haired beggar child, with large startled eyes wide open on a living world.

The tall woman whose statuesque figure had so strangely recalled Teresa's supple, powerful form was holding up the child, propping it on the wall behind her.

Still shaking with the chill terror induced by the vision she now believed she had not seen, Agnes went up closer to the melancholy group.

Even now she longed to hear the woman speak. "Can you tell me the way to Flood Street?" she asked.

The woman looked at her fixedly. "No, that I can't," she said listlessly. "I'm a stranger here." And then, with a passionate energy which startled Agnes, "For God's sake, give me something, lady, to help me to get home! I've walked all the way from Essex; it's taken me, oh! so long with the child, though we've had a lift here and a lift there, and I haven't a penny left. I came to find my husband; but he's lost himself—on purpose!"

A week ago, Agnes Barlow would have shaken her head and passed on. She had always held the theory, carefully inculcated by her careful parents, that it is wrong to give money to beggars in the street.

But perhaps the queer illusion that she had just experienced made her remember Father Ferguson. In a flash she recalled a sermon of the old priest's which had shocked and disturbed his prosperous congregation, for in it the preacher had advanced the astounding theory that it is better to give to nine impostors than to refuse the one just man; nay, more, he had reminded his hearers of the old legend that Christ sometimes comes, in the guise of a beggar, to the wealthy.

She took five shillings out of her purse, and put them, not in the woman's hand, but in that of the little child.

"Thank you," said the woman dully. "May God bless you!" That was all, but Agnes went on, vaguely comforted.

And now at last, helped on her way by more than one good-natured wayfarer, she reached the quiet, but shabby Chelsea street where

Ferrier lived. The fog had drifted towards the river, and in the lamplight Agnes Barlow was not long in finding a large open door, above which was inscribed: "The Thomas More Studios."

Agnes walked timorously through into the square, empty, gas-lit hall, and looked round her with distaste. The place struck her as very ugly and forlorn, utterly lacking in what she had always taken to be the amenities of flat life—an obsequious porter, a lift, electric light.

How strange of Ferrier to have told her that he lived in a building that was beautiful!

Springing in bold and simple curves, rose a wrought-iron staircase, filling up the centre of the narrow, towerlike building. Agnes knew that Ferrier lived high up, somewhere near the top.

She waited a moment at the foot of the staircase. She was gathering up her strength, throwing behind her everything that had meant life, happiness, and—what signified so very much to such a woman as herself—personal repute.

But, even so, Agnes did not falter in her purpose. She was still possessed, driven onward, by a passion of jealous misery.

But, though her spirit was willing, ay, and

more than willing, for revenge, her flesh was weak; and as she began slowly walking up the staircase she started nervously at the grotesque shapes cast by her own shadow, and at the muffled sounds of her own footfalls.

Half-way up the high building the gas-jets burned low, and Agnes felt aggrieved. What a mean, stupid economy on the part of the owners of this strange, unnatural dwelling-place.

How dreadful it would be if she were to meet any one she knew—any one belonging to what she was already unconsciously teaching herself to call her old, happy life! As if in cruel answer to her fear, a door opened, and an old man, clad in a big shabby fur coat and broad-brimmed hat, came out.

Agnes's heart gave a bound in her bosom. Yes; this was what she had somehow thought would happen. In the half-light she took the old man to be an eccentric acquaintance of her father's.

"Mr. Willis?" she whispered hoarsely.

He looked at her, surprised, resentful.

"My name's not Willis," he said gruffly, as he passed her on his way down, and her heart became stilled. How could she have been so foolish as to take that disagreeable old man for kindly-natured Mr. Willis?

She was now very near the top. Only a storey and a half more, and she would be there. Her steps were flagging, but a strange kind of peace had fallen on her. In a few moments she would be safe, for ever, in Ferrier's arms. How strange and unreal the notion seemed!

And then—and then, as if fashioned by some potent incantation from the vaporous fog outside, a tall, grey figure rose out of nothingness, and stood, barring the way, on the steel floor of the landing above her.

Agnes clutched the iron railing, too oppressed rather than too frightened to speak. Out in the fog-laden street she had involuntarily called out the other's name. "Teresa?" she had cried, "Teresa!" But this time no word broke from her lips, for she feared that if she spoke the other would answer.

Teresa Maldo's love, the sisterly love of which Agnes had been so little worthy, had broken down the gateless barrier which stretches its dense length between the living and the dead. What she, the living woman, had not known how to do for Teresa, the dead woman had come back to do for her—for now Agnes seemed suddenly able to measure the depth of the gulf into which she had been about to throw herself. . . .

She stared with fearful, fascinated eyes at

the immobile figure swathed in grey, cere-like garments, and her gaze travelled stealthfully up to the white, passionless face, drained of all expression save that of watchful concern and understanding tenderness. . . .

With a swift movement Agnes turned round. Clinging to the iron rail, she stumbled down the stairway to the deserted hall, and with swift terror-hastened steps rushed out into the street.

Through the fog she plunged, not even sparing a moment to look back and up to the dimly lighted window behind which poor Ferrier stood,—as a softer, a truer-natured woman might have done. Violently she put all thought of her lover from her, and as she hurried along with tightening breath, the instinct of self-preservation alone possessing her, she became more and more absorbed in measuring the fathomless depth of the pit in which she had so nearly fallen.

Her one wish now was to get home—to get home—to get home—before Frank got back.

But the fulfilment of that wish was denied her—for as Agnes Barlow walked, crying softly as she went, in the misty darkness along the road which led from Summerfield station to the gate of The Haven, there fell on her ear the rhythmical tramp of well-shod feet.

She shrank near to the hedge, in no mood to

greet or to accept greeting from a neighbour. But the walker was now close to her. He struck a match.

"Agnes?" It was Frank Barlow's voice—shamed, eager, questioning. "Is that you? I thought—I hoped you would come home by this train."

And as she gave no immediate answer, as he missed—God alone knew with what relief—the prim, cold accents to which his wife had accustomed him of late, he hurried forward and took her masterfully in his arms. "Oh! my darling," he whispered huskily, "I know I've been a beast—but I've never left off loving you—and I can't stand your coldness, Agnes; it's driving me to the devil! Forgive me, my pure angel——"

And Frank Barlow's pure angel did forgive him, and with a spontaneity and generous forgetfulness which he will ever remember. Nay, more; Agnes—and this touched her husband deeply—even gave up her pleasant acquaintance with that writing fellow, Ferrier, because Ferrier, through no fault of his, was associated, in both their minds, with the terrible time each would have given so much to obliterate from the record of their otherwise cloudless married life.

WHY THEY MARRIED

WHY THEY MARRIED

"God doeth all things well, though by what strange, solemn, and murderous contrivances."

JOHN COXETER was sitting with his back to the engine in a first-class carriage in the Paris-Boulogne night train. Not only Englishman, but Englishman of a peculiarly definite class, that of the London civil servant, was written all over his spare, still active figure.

It was late September, and the rush homewards had begun; so Coxeter, being a man of precise and careful habit, had reserved a corner seat. Then, just before the train had started, a certain Mrs. Archdale, a young widowed lady with whom he was acquainted, had come up to him on the Paris platform, and to her he had given up his seat.

Coxeter had willingly made the little sacrifice of his personal comfort, but he had felt annoyed when Mrs. Archdale in her turn had yielded the corner place with foolish altruism to a French lad exchanging vociferous farewells with his parents. When the train started the boy did not give the seat back to the courteous Englishwoman to whom it belonged, and Coxeter, more vexed by the matter than it was worth, would have liked to punch the boy's head.

And yet, as he now looked straight before him, sitting upright in the carriage which was rocking and jolting as only a French railway carriage can rock and jolt, he realized that he himself had gained by the lad's lack of honesty. By having thus given away something which did not belong to her, Mrs. Archdale was now seated, if uncomfortably hemmed in and encompassed on each side, just opposite to Coxeter himself.

Coxeter was well aware that to stare at a woman is the height of bad breeding, but unconsciously he drew a great distinction between what is good taste to do when one is being observed, and that which one does when no one can catch one doing it. Without making the slightest effort, in fact by looking straight before him, Nan Archdale fell into his direct line of vision, and he allowed his eyes to rest on her with an unwilling sense that there was nothing in the world he had rather they rested on. Her appearance pleased his fastidious, rather old-fashioned taste. Mrs. Archdale was wearing a long grey cloak. On her head was poised a dark hat trimmed with Mercury wings; it rested lightly on the pale golden hair which formed so agreeable a contrast to her deep blue eyes.

Coxeter did not believe in luck; the word which means so much to many men had no place in his vocabulary, or even in his imagination. But, still, the sudden appearance of Mrs. Archdale in the great Paris station had been an agreeable surprise, one of those incidents which, just because of their unexpectedness, make a man feel not only pleased with himself, but at one with the world.

Before Mrs. Archdale had come up to the carriage door at which he was standing, several things had contributed to put Coxeter in an ill-humour.

It had seemed to his critical British phlegm that he was surrounded, immersed against his will, in floods of emotion. Among his fellow travellers the French element predominated. Heavens! how they talked—jabbered would be the better word—laughed and cried! How they hugged and embraced one another! Coxeter thanked God he was an Englishman.

His feeling of bored disgust was intensified

by the conduct of a long-nosed, sallow man, who had put his luggage into the same carriage as that where Coxeter's seat had been reserved.

Strange how the peculiar characteristics common to the Jewish race survive, whatever be the accident of nationality. This man also was saying good-bye, his wife being a dark, thin, eager-looking woman of a very common French type. Coxeter looked at them critically, he wondered idly if the woman was Jewish too. On the whole he thought not. She was half crying, half laughing, her hands now clasping her husband's arm, now travelling, with a gesture of tenderness, up to his fleshy face, while he seemed to tolerate rather than respond to her endearments and extravagant terms of affection. "*Adieu, mon petit homme adoré!*" she finally exclaimed, just as the tickets were being examined, and to Coxeter's surprise the adored one answered in a very English voice, albeit the utterance was slightly thick, "There, there! That'ull do, my dear girl. It's only for a fortnight after all."

Coxeter felt a pang of sincere pity for the poor fellow; a cad, no doubt—but an English cad, cursed with an emotional French wife!

Then his attention had been most happily diverted by the unexpected appearance of Mrs. Archdale. She had come up behind him very quietly, and he had heard her speak before actually seeing her. "Mr. Coxeter, are you going back to England, or have you only come to see someone off?"

Not even then had Coxeter—to use a phrase which he himself would not have used, for he avoided the use of slang—"given himself away." Over his lantern-shaped face, across his thin, determined mouth, there had still lingered a trace of the supercilious smile with which he had been looking round him. And, as he had helped Mrs. Archdale into the compartment, as he indicated to her the comfortable seat he had reserved for himself, not even she—noted though she was for her powers of sympathy and understanding—had divined the delicious tremor, the curious state of mingled joy and discomfort into which her sudden presence had thrown the man whom she had greeted a little doubtfully, by no means sure that he would welcome her companionship on a long journey.

And, indeed, in spite of the effect she produced upon him, in spite of the fact that she was the only human being who had ever had, or was ever likely to have, the power of making him feel humble, not quite satisfied with himself—Coxeter disapproved of Mrs. Archdale. At the present moment he disapproved of her rather more than usual, for if she meant to give up that corner seat, why had she not so arranged as to sit by him? Instead, she was now talking to the French boy who occupied what should have been her seat.

But Nan Archdale, as all her friends called her, was always like that. Coxeter never saw her, never met her at the houses to which he went simply in order that he might meet her, without wondering why she wasted so much of the time she might have spent in talking to him, and above all in listening to him, in talking and listening to other people.

Four years ago, not long after their first acquaintance, he had made her an offer of marriage, impelled by something which had appeared at the time quite outside himself and his usual wise, ponderate view of life. He had been relieved, as well as keenly hurt, when she had refused him.

Everything that concerned himself appeared to John Coxeter of such moment and importance that at the time it had seemed incredible that Nan Archdale would be able to keep to herself the peculiar honour which had befallen her,—one, by the way, which Coxeter had never seriously thought of conferring on any other woman. But as time went on he became aware that she had actually kept the secret which was not hers to betray, and, emboldened by the knowledge that she alone knew of his humiliating bondship, he had again, after a certain interval, written and asked her if she would marry him. Again she had refused, in a kind, impersonal little note, and this last time she had gone so far as to declare that in this matter she really knew far better than he did himself what was good for him, and once more something deep in his heart had said "Amen."

When he thought about it, and he went on thinking about it more than was quite agreeable for his own comfort or peace of mind, Coxeter would tell himself, with what he believed to be a vicarious pang of regret, that Mrs. Archdale had made a sad mistake as regarded her own interest. He felt sure she was not fit to live alone; he knew she ought to be surrounded by the kind of care and protection which only a husband can properly bestow on a woman. He, Coxeter, would have known how to detach her from the unsuitable people by whom she was always surrounded.

Nan Archdale, and Coxeter was much concerned that it was so, had an instinctive attraction for those poor souls who lead forlorn hopes, and of whom—they being unsuccessful in their fine endeavours—the world never hears.

She also had a strange patience and tenderness for those ne'er-do-wells of whom even the kindest grow weary after a time. Nan had a mass of queer friends, old protégés for whom she worked unceasingly in a curious, detached fashion, which was quite her own, and utterly apart from any of the myriad philanthropic societies with which the world she lived in, and to which she belonged by birth, interests its prosperous and intelligent leisure.

It was characteristic that Nan's liking for John Coxeter often took the form of asking him to help these queer, unsatisfactory people. Why, even in this last week, while he had been in Paris, he had come into close relation with one of Mrs. Archdale's "odd-come-shorts." This time the man was an inventor, and of all unpractical and useless things he had patented an appliance for saving life at sea!

Nan Archdale had given the man a note to Coxeter, and it was characteristic of the latter that, while resenting what Mrs. Archdale had done, he had been at some pains when in Paris to see the man in question. The invention—as Coxeter had of course known would be the case—was a ridiculous affair, but for Nan's sake he had agreed to submit it to the Admiralty expert whose business it is to consider and pronounce on such futile things.

The queer little model which its maker believed would in time supersede the life-belts now carried on every British ship, had but one merit, it was small and portable : at the present moment it lay curled up, looking like a cross between a serpent's cast skin and a child's spent balloon, in Coxeter's portmanteau. Even while he had accepted the parcel with a coolly civil word of thanks, he had mentally composed the letter with which he would ultimately dash the poor inventor's hopes.

To-night, however, sitting opposite to her, he felt glad that he had been to see the man, and he looked forward to telling her about it. Scarcely consciously to himself, it always made Coxeter glad to feel that he had given Nan pleasure, even pleasure of which he disapproved.

And yet how widely apart were these two people's sympathies and interests! Putting Nan aside, John Coxeter was only concerned with two things in life—his work at the Treasury and himself—and people only interested him in relation to these two major problems of existence. Nan Archdale was a citizen of the world—a freewoman of that dear kingdom of romance which still contains so many fragrant byways and sunny oases for those who have the will to find them. But for her freedom of this kingdom she would have been a very sad woman, oppressed by the griefs and sorrows of that other world to which she also belonged, for Nan's human circle was ever widening, and in her strange heart there seemed always room for those whom others rejected and despised.

She had the power no human being had ever had—that of making John Coxeter jealous. This was the harder to bear inasmuch as he was well aware that jealousy is a very ridiculous human failing, and one with which he had no sympathy or understanding when it affected— as it sometimes did—his acquaintances and colleagues. Fortunately for himself, he was not retrospectively jealous—jealous that is of the dead man of whom certain people belonging to his and to Nan's circle sometimes spoke of as "poor Jim Archdale." Coxeter knew vaguely that Archdale had been a bad lot, though never actually unkind to his wife; nay, more, during the short time their married life had lasted, Archdale, it seemed, had to a certain extent reformed.

Although he was unconscious of it, John Coxeter was a very material human being, and this no doubt was why this woman had so compelling an attraction for him; for Nan Archdale appeared to be all spirit, and that in spite of her eager, sympathetic concern in the lives which circled about hers.

And yet? Yet there was certainly a strong, unspoken link between them, this man and woman who had so little in common the one with the other. They met often, if only because they both lived in Marylebone, that most conventional quarter of old Georgian London, she in Wimpole Street, he in a flat in Wigmore Street. She always was glad to see him, and seemed a little sorry when he left her. Coxeter was one of the rare human beings to whom Nan ever spoke of herself and of her own concerns. But, in spite of that curious kindliness, she did not do what so many people who knew John Coxeter instinctively did—ask his advice, and, what was, of course, more seldom done—take it. In fact he had sometimes angrily told himself that Nan attached no weight to his opinion, and as time had gone on he had almost given up offering her unsought advice.

John Coxeter attached great importance to health. He realized that a perfect physical condition is a great possession, and he took considerable pains to keep himself what he called "fit." Now Mrs. Archdale was recklessly imprudent concerning her health, the health, that is, which was of so great a value to him, her friend. She took her meals at such odd times; she did not seem to mind, hardly to know, what she ate and drank!

Of the many strange things Coxeter had known her to do, by far the strangest, and one which he could scarcely think of without an inward tremor, had happened only a few months ago.

Nan had been with an ailing friend, and the ailing friend's only son, in the Highlands, and this friend, a foolish woman,—when recalling the matter Coxeter never omitted to call this lady a foolish woman—on sending her boy back to school, had given him what she had thought to be a dose of medicine out of the wrong bottle, a bottle marked "Poison." Nothing could be done, for the boy had started on his long railway journey south before the mistake had been discovered, and even Coxeter, when hearing the story told, had realized that had he been there he would have been sorry, really sorry, for the foolish mother.

But Nan's sympathy—and on this point Coxeter always dwelt with a special sense of injury—had taken a practical shape. She had poured out a similar dose from the bottle marked "Poison" and had calmly drunk it, observing as she did so, "I don't believe it *is* poison in the real sense of the word, but at any rate we shall soon be able to find out exactly what is happening to Dick."

Nothing, or at least nothing but a bad headache, had followed, and so far had Nan been justified of her folly. But to Coxeter it was terrible to think of what might have happened, and he had not shared in any degree the mingled amusement and admiration which the story, as told afterwards by the culpable mother, had drawn forth. In fact, so deeply had he felt about it that he had not trusted himself to speak of the matter to Mrs. Archdale.

But Mrs. Archdale was not only reckless of her health; she was also reckless—perhaps uncaring would be the truer word—of something which John Coxeter supposed every nice woman to value even more than her health or appearance, that is the curiously intangible, and yet so easily frayed, human vesture termed reputation.

To John Coxeter the women of his own class, if worthy, that is, of consideration and respect, went clad in a delicate robe of ermine, and the thought that this ermine should have even a shade cast on its fairness was most repugnant to him. Now Nan Archdale was not as careful in this matter of keeping her ermine unspoiled and delicately white as she ought to have been, and this was the stranger inasmuch as even Coxeter realized that there was about his friend a Una-like quality which made her unafraid, because unsuspecting, of evil.

Another of the cardinal points of Coxeter's carefully thought-out philosophy of life was that in this world no woman can touch pitch without being defiled. And yet on one occasion, at least, the woman who now sat opposite to him had proved the falsity of this view. Nan Archdale, apparently indifferent to the opinion of those who wished her well, had allowed herself to be closely associated with one of those unfortunate members of her own sex who, at certain intervals in the history of the civilized world, become heroines of a drama of which each act takes place in the Law Courts. Of these dramas every whispered word, every piece of "business"—to pursue the analogy to its logical end—is overheard and visualized not by thousands but by millions,—in fact by all those of an age to read a newspaper.

Had the woman in the case been Mrs. Archdale's sister, Coxeter with a groan would have admitted that she owed her a duty, though a duty which he would fain have had her shirk or rather delegate to another. But this woman was no sister, not even a friend, simply an old acquaintance known to Nan, 'tis true, over many years. Nan had done what she had done, had taken her in and sheltered her, going to the Court with her every day, simply because there seemed absolutely no one else willing to do it.

When he had first heard of what Mrs. Archdale was undertaking to do, Coxeter had been so dismayed that he had felt called upon to expostulate with her.

Very few words had passed between them. "Is it possible," he had asked, "that you think her innocent? That you believe her own story?"

To this Mrs. Archdale had answered with some distress, "I don't know, I haven't thought about it—— As she says she is—I hope she is. If she's not, I'd rather not know it."

It had been a confused utterance, and somehow she had made him feel sorry that he had said anything. Afterwards, to his surprise and unwilling relief, he discovered that Mrs. Archdale had not suffered in reputation as he had expected her to do. But it made him feel, more than ever, that she needed a strong, wise man to take care of her, and to keep her out of the mischief into which her unfortunate good-nature—that was the way Coxeter phrased it to himself—was so apt to lead her.

It was just after this incident that he had again asked her to marry him, and that she had again refused him. But it was since then that he had become really her friend.

At last Mrs. Archdale turned away, or else the French boy had come to an end of his eloquence. Perhaps she would now lean a little forward and speak to him—the friend whom she had not seen for some weeks and whom she had seemed so sincerely glad to see half an hour ago? But no; she remained silent, her face full of thought.

Coxeter leant back; as a rule he never read in a train, for he was aware that it is injurious to the eyesight to do so. But to-night he suddenly told himself that after all he might just as well look at the English paper he had bought at the station. He might at least see what sort of crossing they were going to have to-night. Not that he minded for himself. He was a good sailor and always stayed on deck whatever the weather, but he hoped it would be smooth for Mrs. Archdale's sake. It was so unpleasant for a lady to have a rough passage.

Again, before opening the paper, he glanced

across at her. She did not look strong; that air of delicacy, combined as it was with perfect health—for Mrs. Archdale was never ill—was one of the things that made her attractive to John Coxeter. When he was with a woman, he liked to feel that he was taking care of her, and that she was more or less dependent on his good offices. Somehow or other he always felt this concerning Nan Archdale, and that even when she was doing something of which he disapproved and which he would fain have prevented her doing.

Coxeter turned round so that the light should fall on the page at which he had opened his newspaper, which, it need hardly be said, was the *Morning Post.* Presently there came to him the murmuring of two voices, Mrs. Archdale's clear, low utterances, and another's, guttural and full.

Ah! then he had been right; the fellow sitting there, on Nan's other side, was a Jew: probably something financial, connected with the Stock Exchange. Coxeter of the Treasury looked at the man he took to be a financier with considerable contempt. Coxeter prided himself on his knowledge of human beings,— or rather of men, for even his self-satisfaction did not go so far as to make him suppose that he entirely understood women; there had been a time when he had thought so, but that was a long while ago.

He began reading his newspaper. There was a most interesting article on education. After having glanced at this, he studied more carefully various little items of social news which reminded him that he had been away from London for some weeks. Then, as he read on, the conversation between Nan Archdale and the man next to her became more audible to him. All the other people in the carriage were French, and so first one, and then the other, window had been closed.

His ears had grown accustomed to the muffled, thundering sounds caused by the train, and gradually he became aware that Nan Archdale was receiving some singular confidences from the man with whom she was now speaking. The fellow was actually unrolling before her the whole of his not very interesting life, and by degrees Coxeter began rather to overhear than to listen consciously to what was being said.

The Jew, though English by birth, now lived in France. As a young man he had failed in business in London, and then he had made a fresh start abroad, apparently impelled thereto by his great affection for his mother. The Jewish race, so Coxeter reminded himself, are admirable in every relation of private life, and it was apparently in order that his mother might not have to alter her style of living that the person on whom Mrs. Archdale was now fixing her attention had finally accepted a post in a Paris house of business— no, not financial, something connected with the sweetmeat trade.

Coxeter gathered that the speaker had at last saved enough money to make a start for himself, and that now he was very prosperous. He spoke of what he had done with legitimate pride, and when describing the struggle he had gone through, the fellow used a very odd expression, "It wasn't all jam!" he said. Now he was in a big way of business, going over to London every three months, partly in connection with his work, partly to see his old mother.

Behind his newspaper Coxeter told himself that it was amazing any human being should tell so much of his private concerns to a stranger. Even more amazing was it that a refined, rather peculiar, woman like Nan Archdale should care to listen to such a commonplace story. But listening she was, saying a word here and there, asking, too, very quaint, practical questions concerning the sweetmeat trade. Why, even Coxeter became interested in spite of himself, for the Jew was an intelligent man, and as he talked on Coxeter learned with surprise that there is a romantic and exciting side even to making sweets.

"What a pity it is," he heard Nan say at last in her low, even voice, "that you can't now come back to England and settle down there. Surely it would make your mother much happier, and you don't seem to like Paris so very much?"

"That is true," said the man, "but—well, unluckily there's an obstacle to my doing that——"

Coxeter looked up from his paper. The stranger's face had become troubled, pre-occupied, and his eyes were fixed, or so Coxeter fancied them to be, on Nan Archdale's left hand, the slender bare hand on which the only ring was her wedding ring.

Coxeter once more returned to his paper, but for some minutes he made no attempt to follow the dancing lines of print.

"I trust you won't be offended if I ask whether you are, or are not, a married lady?" The sweetmeat man's voice had a curious note of shamed interrogation threading itself through the words.

Coxeter felt surprised and rather shocked. This was what came of allowing oneself to become familiar with an underbred stranger! But

Nan had apparently not so taken the impertinent question, for, "I am a widow," Coxeter heard her answer gently, in a voice that had no touch of offence in it.

And then, after a few moments, staring with frowning eyes at the spread-out sheet of newspaper before him, Coxeter, with increasing distaste and revolt, became aware that Mrs. Archdale was now receiving very untoward confidences—confidences which Coxeter had always imagined were never made save under the unspoken seal of secrecy by one man to another. This objectionable stranger was telling Nan Archdale the story of the woman who had seen him off at the station, and whose absurd phrase, "*Adieu, mon petit homme adoré,*" had rung so unpleasantly in his, Coxeter's, ears.

The eavesdropper was well aware that such stories are among the everyday occurrences of life, but his knowledge was largely theoretical; John Coxeter was not the sort of man to whom other men are willing to confide their shames, sorrows, or even successes in a field of which the aftermath is generally bitter.

In as far as such a tale can be told with decent ambiguity it was so told by this man of whose refinement Coxeter had formed so poor an opinion, but still the fact that he was telling it remained—and it was a fact which to such a man as Coxeter constituted an outrage on the decencies of life.

Mrs. Archdale, by her foolish good-nature, had placed herself in such a position as to be consulted in a case of conscience concerning a Jewish tradesman and his light o' love, and now the man was debating with her as with himself, as to whether he should marry this woman, as to whether he should force on his respectable English mother a French daughter-in-law of unmentionable antecedents! Coxeter gathered that the liaison had lasted ten years —that it had begun, in fact, very soon after the man had first come to Paris.

In addition to his feeling of wrath that Nan Archdale should become cognisant of so sordid a tale, there was associated a feeling of shame that he, Coxeter, had overheard what it had not been meant that he should hear.

Perforce the story went on to its melancholy and inconclusive end, and then, suddenly, Coxeter became possessed with a desire to see Nan Archdale's face. He glanced across at her. To his surprise her face was expressionless; but her left hand was no longer lying on her knee, it was supporting her chin, and she was looking straight before her.

"I suppose," she said at last, "that you

have made a proper provision for your—your friend? I mean in case of your death. I hope you have so arranged matters that if anything should happen to you, this poor woman who loves you would not have to go back to the kind of life from which you took her." Even Coxeter divined that Nan had not found it easy to say this thing.

"Why, no, I haven't done anything of that sort. I never thought of doing it; she's always been the delicate party. I am as strong as a horse!"

"Still—still, life's very uncertain." Mrs. Archdale was now looking straight into the face of the stranger on whom she was thrusting unsought advice.

"She has no claim on me, none at all——" the man spoke defensively. "I don't think she'd expect anything of that sort. She's had a very good time with me. After all, I haven't treated her badly."

"I'm sure you haven't," Nan spoke very gently. "I am sure you have been always kind to her. But, if I may use the simile you used just now, life, even to the happiest, the most sheltered, of women, isn't all jam!"

The man looked at her with a doubting, shame-faced glance. "I expect you're right," he said abruptly. "I ought to have thought of it. I'll make my will when I'm in England this time—I ought to have done so before."

Suddenly Coxeter leant forward. He felt the time had come when he really must put an end to this most unseemly conversation.

"Mrs. Archdale?" he spoke loudly, insistently. She looked up, startled at the sharpness of the tone, and the man next her, whose eyes had been fixed on her face with so moved and doubting a look, sat back. "I want to tell you that I've seen your inventor, and that I've promised to put his invention before the right quarter at the Admiralty."

In a moment Nan was all eagerness. "It really is a very wonderful thing," she said; "I'm so grateful, Mr. Coxeter. Did you go and see it tried? *I* did, last time I was in Paris; the man took me to a swimming-bath on the Seine—such an odd place—and there he tested it before me. I was really very much impressed. I do hope you will say a word for it. I am sure they would value your opinion."

Coxeter looked at her rather grimly. "No, I didn't see it tested." To think that she should have wasted even an hour of her time in such a foolish manner, and in such a queer place, too! "I didn't see the use of doing so, though of course the man was very anxious

I should. I'm afraid the thing's no good. How could it be?" He smiled superciliously, and he saw her redden.

"How unfair that is!" she exclaimed. "How can you possibly tell whether it's no good if you haven't seen it tried? Now I *have* seen the thing tried."

There was such a tone of protest in her voice that Coxeter felt called upon to defend himself. "I daresay the thing's all right in theory," he said quickly, "and I believe what he says about the ordinary life-belts; it's quite true, I mean, that they drown more people than they save: but that's only because people don't know how to put them on. This thing's a toy—not practical at all." He spoke more irritably than he generally allowed himself to speak, for he could see that the Jew was listening to all that they were saying.

All at once, Mrs. Archdale actually included the sweetmeat stranger in their conversation, and Coxeter at last found himself at her request most unwillingly taking the absurd model out of his bag. "Of course you've got to imagine this in a rough sea," he said sulkily, playing the devil's advocate, "and not in a fresh water river bath."

"Well, *I* wouldn't mind trying it in a rough sea, Mr. Coxeter." Nan smiled as she spoke.

Coxeter wondered if she was really serious. Sometimes he suspected that Mrs. Archdale was making fun of him—but that surely was impossible.

II

When at last they reached Boulogne and went on board the packet, Coxeter's ill-humour vanished. It was cold, raw, and foggy, and most of their fellow-passengers at once hurried below, but Mrs. Archdale decided to stay on the upper deck. This pleased her companion; now at last he would have her to himself.

In his precise and formal way he went to a good deal of trouble to make Nan comfortable; and she, so accustomed to take thought for others, stood aside and watched him find a sheltered corner, secure with some difficulty a deck chair, and then defend it with grim determination against two or three people who tried to lay hands upon it.

At last he beckoned to her to sit down. "Where's your rug?" he asked. She answered meekly, "I haven't brought one."

He put his own rug,—large, light, warm, the best money could buy—round her knees; and in the pleasure it gave him to wait on her thus he did not utter aloud the reproof which had been on his lips. But she saw him shake his head over a more unaccountable omission—on the journey she had somehow lost her gloves. He took his own off, and with a touch of masterfulness made her put them on, himself fastening the big bone buttons over each of her small, childish wrists; but his manner while he did all these things—he would have scorned himself had it been otherwise—was impersonal, businesslike.

There are men whose every gesture in connection with a woman becomes an instinctive caress. Such men, as every woman learns in time, are not good "stayers," but they make the time go by very quickly—sometimes.

With Coxeter every minute lasted sixty seconds. But Nan Archdale found herself looking at him with unwonted kindliness. At last she said, a little tremulously, and with a wondering tone in her voice, "You're very kind to me, Mr. Coxeter." Those who spend their lives in speeding others on their way are generally allowed to trudge along alone; so at least this woman had found it to be. Coxeter made no answer to her words—perhaps he did not hear them.

Even in the few minutes which had elapsed since they came on board, the fog had deepened. The shadowy figures moving about the deck only took substance when they stepped into the circle of brightness cast by a swinging globe of light which hung just above Nan Archdale's head. Coxeter moved forward and took up his place in front of the deck-chair, protecting its occupant from the jostling of the crowd, for the sheltered place he had found stood but a little way back from the passage between the land gangway and the iron staircase leading to the lower deck.

There were more passengers that night than usual. They passed, a seemingly endless procession, moving slowly out of the darkness into the circle of light and then again into the white, engulfing mist.

At last the deck became clear of moving figures; the cold, raw fog had driven almost everyone below. But Coxeter felt curiously content, rather absurdly happy. This was to him a great adventure. . . .

He took out his watch. If the boat started to time they would be off in another five minutes. He told himself that this was turning out a very pleasant journey; as a rule when crossing the Channel one meets tiresome people one knows, and they insist on talking to one. And then, just as he was thinking this, there suddenly surged forward out of the foggy mist two people, a newly married couple named Rendel, with whom both he and Mrs. Archdale were acquainted, at whose wedding indeed they had both been present some six or seven weeks ago. So absorbed in earnest talk with one another were the bride and bridegroom that they did not seem to see where they were going; but when close to Mrs. Archdale they stopped short, and turned towards one another, still talking so eagerly as to be quite oblivious of possible eavesdroppers.

John Coxeter, standing back in the shadow, felt a sudden gust of envious pain. They were evidently on their way home from their honeymoon, these happy young people, blessed with good looks, money, health, and love; their marriage had been the outcome of quite a pretty romance.

But stay,—what was this they were saying? Both he and Nan unwillingly heard the quick interchange of words, the wife's shrill, angry utterances, the husband's good-humoured expostulations. "I won't stay on the boat, Bob. I don't see why we should risk our lives in order that you may be back in town to-morrow. I know it's not safe—my great-uncle, the Admiral, always said that the worst storm at sea was not as bad as quite a small fog!" Then the gruff answer: "My dear child, don't be a fool! The boat wouldn't start if there was the slightest danger. You heard what that man told us. The fog was much worse this morning, and the boat was only an hour late!" "Well, you can do as you like, but *I* won't cross to-night. Where's the use of taking any risk? Mother's uncle, the Admiral——" and Coxeter heard with shocked approval the man's "Damn your great-uncle, the Admiral!"

There they stood, not more than three yards off, the pretty, angry little spitfire looking up at her indignant, helpless husband. Coxeter, if disgusted, was amused; there was also the comfort of knowing that they would certainly pretend not to see him, even if by chance they recognized him, intent as they were on their absurd difference.

"I shall go back and spend the night at the station hotel. No, you needn't trouble to find Stockton for me—there's no time." Coxeter and Nan heard the laughing gibe, "Then you don't mind your poor maid being drowned as well as your poor husband," but the bride went on as if he hadn't spoken—"I've quite enough money with me; you needn't give me anything—*good-bye*."

She disappeared into the fog in the direction of the gangway, and Coxeter moved hastily to one side. He wished to save Bob Rendel the annoyance of recognizing him; but then, with amazing suddenness, something happened which made Coxeter realize that after all women were even more inexplicable, unreasonable beings than even he had always known them to be.

There came the quick patter of feet over the damp deck, and Mrs. Rendel was back again, close to where her husband was standing.

"I've made up my mind to stay on the boat," she said quietly. "I think you are very unwise, as well as very obstinate, to cross in this fog; but if you won't give way, then I'd rather be with you, and share the danger."

Bob Rendel laughed, not very kindly, and together they went across to the stair leading below.

Coxeter opened his mouth to speak, then he closed it again. What a scene! What a commentary on married life! And these two people were supposed to be "in love" with one another.

The little episode had shocked him, jarred his contentment. "If you don't mind, I'll go and smoke a pipe," he said stiffly.

Mrs. Archdale looked up. "Oh yes, please do," and yet she felt suddenly bereft of something warm, enveloping, kindly. The words formed themselves on her lips, "Don't go too far away," but she did not speak them aloud. But, as if in answer to her unspoken request, Coxeter called out, "I'm just here, close by, if you want anything," and the commonplace words gave her a curious feeling of security,— a feeling, though she herself was unaware of it, which her own care and tenderness for others often afforded to those round whom she threw the sheltering mantle of her kindness.

Perhaps because he was so near, John Coxeter remained in her thoughts. Almost alone of those human beings with whom life brought her in contact, he made no demand on her sympathy, and very little on her time. In fact, his first offer of marriage had taken her so much by surprise as to strike her as slightly absurd; she had also felt it, at the time, to be an offence, for she had given him no right to encroach on the inner shrine of her being.

Trying to account for what he had done, she had supposed that John Coxeter, being a man who evidently ordered his life according to some kind of system, had believed himself ripe for the honourable estate of marriage, and had chosen her as being "suitable."

When writing her cold letter of refusal, she had expected to hear within a few weeks of his engagement to some "nice" girl. But time had gone by and nothing of the sort had happened. Coxeter's second offer, conveyed, as had been the first, in a formal letter, had found her in a very different mood, for it had followed very closely on that done by her of which he, John Coxeter, had so greatly disapproved. She had been touched this second time and not at all offended, and gradually they had become friends. It was after his second offer that Nan began making use of him, not so much for herself as on behalf of other people.

Nan Archdale led her life without reference to what those about her considered appropriate or desirable; and years had gone by since the boldest busybody among them would have ventured a word of rebuke. Her social background was composed of happy, prosperous people. They had but little to do with her, however, save when by some amazing mischance things went wrong with them; when all went well they were apt to forget Nan Archdale. But John Coxeter, though essentially one of them by birth and instinct, and though it had been through them that she had first met him, never forgot her.

Yet though they had become, in a sense, intimate, he made on her none of those demands which endear a man to a woman. Living up on a pleasant tableland of self-approval, he never touched the heights or depths which go to form the relief map of most human beings' lives. He always did his duty and generally enjoyed doing it, and he had no patience, only contempt, for those who shirked theirs.

The passion of love, that greatest of the Protean riddles set by nature to civilized man and woman, played no part, or so Nan Archdale believed, in John Coxeter's life. At the time she had received the letter in which he had first asked her to marry him, there had come to her, seen through the softening mists of time, a sharp, poignant remembrance of Jim Archdale's offer, "If you won't have me, Nan, I'll do something desperate! You'll be sorry then!" So poor Jim Archdale had conquered her; and looking back, when she recalled their brief married life, she forgot the selfishness and remembered only the love, the love which had made Jim so dependent on her presence and her sympathy.

But if John Coxeter were incapable of love, she now knew him to be a good friend, and it was the friend—so she believed, and was grateful to him for it,—who had asked her to accept what he had quixotically supposed would be the shelter of his name when she had done that thing of which he had disapproved.

To-night Nan could not help wondering if he would ever again ask her to marry him. She thought not—she hoped not. She told herself quite seriously that he was one of those men who are far happier unwedded. His standard, not so much of feminine virtue as of feminine behaviour, was too high. Take what had happened just now; she had listened indulgently, tenderly, to the quarrel of the newly married couple, but she had seen the effect it had produced on John Coxeter. To him it had been a tragedy, and an ugly, ignoble tragedy to boot.

The deck was now clear of passengers. Out in the open sea the fog had become so thick as to be impenetrable, and the boat seemed to be groping its way, heralded by the mournful screaming of the siren. Mrs. Archdale felt drowsy; she leant back and closed her eyes. Coxeter was close by, puffing steadily at his pipe. She felt a pleasant sensation of security.

She was roused, rather startled, by a man bending over her, while a voice said gruffly, "I think, ma'am, that you'd better get into shelter. The deck saloon is close by. Allow me to lead you to it."

Nan rose obediently. With the petty officer on one side and Coxeter on the other, she made a slow progress across the deck, and so to the large, brilliantly lighted saloon. There the fog had been successfully shut out, and some fifteen to twenty people sat on the velvet benches; among them was the sweetmeat merchant to whom Nan had talked in the train.

Coxeter found a comfortable place for Nan rather apart from the others, and sitting down he began to talk to her. The fog-horn, which was trumpeting more loudly, more insistently than ever, did not, he thought, interfere with their conversation as much as it might have done.

"We shan't be there till morning," Coxeter heard a man say, "till morning doth appear, at this rate!"

"I suppose we're all right. There's no *real* danger in a fog—not in the Channel; there never has been an accident on the Channel passage—not an accident of any serious kind."

"Yes, there was—to one of the Dieppe boats—a very bad accident!"

And then several of those present joined in the discussion. The man who had recalled the Dieppe boat accident could be heard, self-assertive, pragmatical, his voice raised above the voices around him. "I've been all over the world in my time, and when I'm caught in a fog at sea I always get up, dress, and go up on deck, however sleepy I may be."

Coxeter, sitting apart by Nan's side, listened with some amusement. His rather thin sense of humour was roused by the fact that the people around him were talking in so absurd a manner. This delay was not pleasant; it might even mean that he would be a few hours late at the Treasury, a thing he had never once been after a holiday, for Coxeter prided himself on his punctuality in the little as well as the great things of life. But, of course, all traffic in the Channel would be delayed by this fog, and his absence would be accounted for by the fact.

Sitting there, close to Mrs. Archdale, with no one sufficiently near to attract her attention, or, what was more likely, to appeal to her for sympathy, he felt he could well afford to wait till the fog cleared off. As for the loud, insistent screaming of the siren, that sound which apparently got on the nerves of most of those present in the deck saloon, of course it was a disagreeable noise, but then they all knew it was a necessary precaution, so why make a fuss about it?

Coxeter turned and looked at his companion, and as he looked at her he felt a little possessive thrill of pride. Mrs. Archdale alone among the people there seemed content and at ease, indeed she was now smiling, smiling very brightly and sweetly, and, following the direction of her eyes, he saw that they rested on a child lying asleep in its mother's arms. . . .

Perhaps after all it was a good thing that Nan was so detached from material things. Before that burst of foolish talk provoked by the fog, he had been speaking to her about a matter very interesting to himself—something connected with his work, something, by the way, of which he would not have thought of speaking to any other woman ; but then Mrs. Archdale, as Coxeter had good reason to know, was exceptionally discreet. . . . She had evidently been very much interested in all he had told her, and he had enjoyed the conversation.

Coxeter became dimly conscious of what it would mean to him to have Nan to come back to when work, and the couple of hours he usually spent at his club, were over. Perhaps if Nan were waiting for him, he would not wish to stay as long as two hours at his club. But then of course he would want Nan all to himself. Jealous? Certainly not. He was far too sensible a man to feel jealous, but he would expect his wife to put him first—

a very long way in front of anybody else. It might be old-fashioned, but he was that sort of man.

Coxeter's thoughts leapt back into the present with disagreeable abruptness. Their Jewish fellow-traveller, the man who had thrust on Mrs. Archdale such unseemly confidences, had got up. He was now heading straight for the place where Mrs. Archdale was sitting.

Coxeter quickly decided that the fellow must not be allowed to bore Mrs. Archdale. She was in his, Coxeter's, care to-night, and he alone had a right to her interest and attention. So he got up and walked down the saloon. To his surprise the other, on seeing him come near, stopped dead. "I want to speak to you," he said in a low voice, "Mr.—er—Coxeter."

Coxeter looked at him, surprised, then reminded himself that his full name, "John Coxeter," was painted on his portmanteau. Also that Mrs. Archdale had called him "Mr. Coxeter" at least once, when discussing that life-saving toy. Still, sharp, observant fellows, Jews! One should always be on one's guard with them. "Yes?" he said interrogatively.

"Well, Mr. Coxeter, I want to ask you to

do me a little favour. The truth is I've just made my will—only a few lines—and I want you to be my second witness. I've no objection, none in the world, to your seeing what I want you to witness."

He spoke very deliberately, as if he had prepared the form of words in which he made his strange request, and as he spoke he held out a sheet of paper apparently torn out of a notebook. "I asked that gentleman over there"—he jerked his thumb over his shoulder—"to be my first witness, and he kindly consented. I'd be much obliged if you'd sign your name just here. I'll also ask you to take charge of it—only a small envelope, as you see. It's addressed to my mother. I've made her executor and residuary legatee."

Coxeter felt a strong impulse to refuse. He never mixed himself up with other people's affairs; he always refused to do so on principle.

The man standing opposite to him divined what was passing through his mind, and broke in, "Only just while we're on this boat. You can tear it up and chuck the pieces away once we're on land again—" he spoke nervously, and with contemptuous amazement Coxeter told himself that the fellow was *afraid*. "Surely you don't think there's any danger?"

he asked. "D'you mean you've made this will because you think something may happen to the boat?"

The other nodded, "Accidents do happen"; he smiled rather foolishly as he said the words, pronouncing the last one, as Coxeter noted with disapproval, "habben." He was holding out a fountain pen; he had an ingratiating manner, and Coxeter, to his own surprise, suddenly gave way.

"All right," he said, and taking the paper in his hand he glanced over it. He had no desire to pry into any man's private affairs, but he wasn't going to sign anything without first reading it.

This odd little will consisted of only two sentences, written in a clear, clerkly hand The first bequeathed an annuity of £240 (six thousand francs) to Léonie Lenoir, of Rue Lafayette, Paris; the second appointed the testator's mother, Mrs. Solomon Munich, of Scott Terrace, Maida Vale, residuary legatee and executor. The will was signed "Victor Munich."

"Very well, I'll sign it," said Coxeter, at last, "and I'll take charge of it till we're on land. But look here—I won't keep it a moment longer!" Then, perhaps a little ashamed of his ungraciousness, "I say, Mr.

Munich, if I were you I'd go below and take a stiffish glass of brandy and water. I once had a fright, I was nearly run over by a brewer's dray at Charing Cross, and I did that—took some brandy I mean—" he jerked the words out, conscious that the other's sallow face had reddened.

Then he signed his name at the bottom of the sheet of paper, and busied himself with putting the envelope carefully into his pocket-book. "There," he said, with the slight supercilious smile which was his most marked physical peculiarity, but of which he was quite unconscious, "your will is quite safe now! If we meet at Folkestone I'll hand it you back; if we miss one another in the—er—fog I'll destroy it, as arranged."

He turned and began walking back to where Nan Archdale was sitting. What a very odd thing! How extraordinary, how unexpected!

Then a light broke in on him. Why, of course, it was Nan who had brought this about! She had touched up the Jew fellow's conscience, frightened him about that woman —the woman who had so absurdly termed him her "*petit homme adoré.*" That's what came of mixing up in other people's business; but Coxeter's eyes nevertheless rested on the sitting figure of his friend with a certain curious indulgence. Odd, sentimental, sensitive creatures—women! But brave—not lacking in moral courage anyway.

As he came close up to her, Mrs. Archdale moved a little, making room for him to sit down by her. It was a graceful, welcoming gesture, and John Coxeter's pulse began to quicken. . . . He told himself that this also was an extraordinary thing—this journey with the woman he had wished to make his wife. He felt her to be so tantalizingly near, and yet in a sense so very far away.

His eyes fell on her right hand, still encased in his large brown glove. As he had buttoned that glove, he had touched her soft wrist, and a wild impulse had come to him to bend yet a little closer and press his lips to the white triangle of yielding flesh. Of course he had resisted the temptation, reminding himself sternly that it was a caddish thing even to have thought of taking advantage of Nan's confiding friendliness. Yet now he wondered whether he had been a fool not to do it. Other men did those things.

There came a dragging, grating sound, the boat shuddering as if in response. Coxeter had the odd sensation that he was being gently but irresistibly pushed round, and yet he sat quite still, with nothing in the saloon changed in relation to himself.

Someone near him exclaimed in a matter-of-fact voice, "We've struck; we're on a rock." Everyone stood up, and he saw an awful look of doubt, of unease, cross the faces of the men and women about him.

The fog-horn ceased trumpeting, and there rose confused sounds, loud hoarse shouts and thin shrill cries, accompanying the dull thunder caused by the tramping of feet. Then the lights went out, all but the yellow flame of a small oil lamp which none of them had known was there.

The glass-panelled door opened widely, and a burly figure holding a torch, which flared up in the still, moist air, was outlined against the steamy waves of fog.

"Come out of here!" he cried; and then, as some people tried to push past him, "Steady, keep cool! There'll be room in the boats for every soul on board," and Coxeter, looking at the pale, glistening face, told himself that the man was lying, and that he knew he lied.

They stumbled out, one by one, and joined the great company which was now swarming over the upper deck, each man and woman forlorn and lonely as human beings must ever be when individually face to face with death.

Coxeter's right hand gripped firmly Mrs. Archdale's arm. She was pressing closely to his side, shrinking back from the rough crowd surging about them, and he was filled with a fierce protective tenderness which left no room in his mind for any thought of self. His one thought was how to preserve his companion from contact with some of those about them; wild-eyed, already distraught creatures, swayed with a terror which set them apart from the mass of quiet, apparently dazed people who stood patiently waiting to do what they were told.

Close to Nan and Coxeter two men were talking Spanish; they were gesticulating, and seemed to be disagreeing angrily as to what course to pursue. Presently one of them suddenly produced a long knife which glittered in the torchlight; with it he made a gesture as if to show the other that he meant to cut his way through the crowd towards the spot, now railed off with rope barriers, where the boats were being got ready for the water.

With a quick movement Coxeter unbuttoned his cloak and drew Nan within its folds; putting his arms round her he held her, loosely and yet how firmly clasped to his breast. "I can't help it," he muttered apologetically. "Forgive me!" As only answer she seemed to draw yet closer to him, and then she lay, still and silent, within his sheltering arms,—and at that moment he remembered to be glad he had not kissed her wrist.

They two stood there, encompassed by a living wall, and yet how strangely alone. The fog had become less dense, or else the resin torches which flared up all about them cleared the air.

From the captain's bridge there whistled every quarter minute a high rocket, and soon from behind the wall of fog came in answer distant signals full of a mingled mockery and hope to the people waiting there.

But for John Coxeter the drama of his own soul took precedence of that going on round him. Had he been alone he would have shared to the full the awful, exasperating feeling of being trapped, of there being nothing to be done, which possessed all the thinking minds about him. But he was not alone——

Nan, lying on his breast, seemed to pour virtue into him—to make him extraordinarily alive. Never had he felt death, extinction so near, and yet there seemed to be something outside himself, a spirit informing, uplifting, and conquering the flesh.

Perceptions, sympathies, which had lain dormant during the whole of his thirty-nine years of life, now sprang into being. His imagination awoke. He saw that it was this woman, now standing, with such complete trust in the niceness of his honour, heart to heart with him, who had made the best of that at once solitary and companioned journey which we call life. He had thought her to be a fool; he now saw that, if a fool, she had been a divine fool, ever engaged while on her pilgrimage with the only things that now mattered. How great was the sum of her achievement compared with his. She had been a beacon diffusing light and warmth; he a shadow among shadows. If to-night he were engulfed in the unknown, for so death was visioned by John Coxeter, who would miss him, who would feel the poorer for his sudden obliteration?

Coxeter came back into the present; he looked round him, and for the first time he felt the disabling clutch of physical fear. The lifebelts were being given out, and there came to him a horrid vision of the people round him as they might be an hour hence, drowned, heads down, legs up, done to death by those monstrous yellow bracelets which they were now putting on with such clumsy, feverish eagerness.

He was touched on the arm, and a husky voice, with which he was by now familiar, said urgently, "Mr. Coxeter—see, I've brought your bag out of the saloon." The man whose name he knew to be Victor Munich was standing at his elbow. "Look here, don't take offence, Mr. Coxeter, I think better of the——" he hesitated—"the life-saver that you've got in this bag of yours than you do. I'm willing to give you a fancy price for it—what would you say to a thousand pounds? I daresay I shan't have occasion to use it, but of course I take that risk."

Coxeter, with a quick, unobtrusive movement, released Mrs. Archdale. He turned and stared, not pleasantly, at the man who was making him so odd an offer. Damn the fellow's impudence! "The life-saver is not for sale," he said shortly.

Nan had heard but little of the quick colloquy. She did not connect it with the fact that the strong protecting arms which had been about her were now withdrawn,—and the tears came into her eyes. She felt both in a physical and in a spiritual sense suddenly alone. John Coxeter, the one human being who ever attempted to place himself on a more intimate, personal plane with her, happened, by a strange irony of fate, to be her companion in this awful adventure. But even he had now turned away from her. . . .

Nay, that was not quite true. He was again looking down at her, and she felt his hand groping for hers. As he found and clasped it, he made a movement as if he wished again to draw her towards him. Gently she resisted, and at once she felt that he responded to her feeling of recoil, and Nan, with a confused sense of shame and anger, was now hurt by his submission. Most men in his place would have made short work of her resistance,—would have taken her, masterfully, into the shelter of his arms.

There came a little stir among the people on the deck. Coxeter heard a voice call out in would-be-cheery tones, "Now then, ladies! Please step out—ladies and children only. Look sharp!" A sailor close by whispered gruffly to his mate, "I'll stick to her anyhow. No crowded boats for me! I expect she'll be a good hour settling—perhaps a bit longer."

As the first boat-load swung into the water, some of the people about them gave a little cheer. Coxeter thought, but he will never be quite sure, that in that cheer Nan joined. There was a delay of a minute; then again the captain's voice rang out, this time in a sharper, more peremptory tone, "Now, ladies, look sharp! Come along, please."

Coxeter unclasped Nan's hand—he did not

know how tightly he had been holding it. He loved her. God, how he loved her! And now he must send her away—away into the shrouding fog—away, just as he had found her. If what he had overheard were true, might he not be sending Nan to a worse fate than that of staying to take the risk with him?

But the very man who had spoken so doubtfully of the boats just now came forward. "You'd best hurry your lady forward, sir. There's no time to lose." There was an anxious, warning note in the rough voice.

"You must go now," said Coxeter heavily. "I shall be all right, Mrs. Archdale," for she was making no movement forward. "There'll be plenty of room for the men in the next boat. I'd walk across the deck with you, but I'm afraid they won't allow that." He spoke in his usual matter-of-fact, rather dry tone, and Nan looked up at him doubtingly. Did he really wish her to leave him?

Flickering streaks of light fell on his face. It was convulsed with feeling,—with what had become an agony of renunciation. She withdrew her eyes, feeling a shamed, exultant pang of joy. "I'll wait till there's room for you, too, Mr. Coxeter." She breathed rather than actually uttered the words aloud.

Another woman standing close by was saying

the same thing to her companion, but in far more eager, more vociferous tones. "Is it likely that I should go away now and leave you, Bob? Of course not—don't be ridiculous!" But the Rendels pushed forward, and finally both found places in this, the last boat but one.

Victor Munich was still standing close to John Coxeter, and Mrs. Archdale, glancing at his sallow, terror-stricken face, felt a thrill of generous pity for the man. "Mr. Coxeter," she whispered, "do give him that life-saver! Did he not ask you for it just now? We don't want it."

Coxeter bent down and unstrapped his portmanteau. He handed to Nan the odd, toy-like thing by which he had set so little store, but which now he let go with a touch of reluctance. He saw her move close to the man whose name she did not know. "Here is the life-saver," she said kindly; "I heard you say you would like it."

"But you?"—he stammered—"how about you?"

"I don't want it. I shall be all right. I shouldn't put it on in any case."

He took it then, avidly; and they saw him go forward with a quick, stealthy movement to the place where the last boat was being got ready for the water.

"There's plenty of room for you and the lady now, sir!" Coxeter hurried Nan across the deck, but suddenly they were pushed roughly back. The rope barriers had been cut, and a hand-to-hand struggle was taking place round the boat,—an ugly scrimmage to which as little reference as possible was made at the wreck inquiry afterwards. To those who looked on it was a horrible, an unnerving sight; and this time Coxeter with sudden strength took Nan back into his arms. He felt her trembling, shuddering against him,— what she had just seen had loosed fear from its leash.

"I'm frightened," she moaned. "Oh, Mr. Coxeter, I'm so horribly frightened of those men! Are they all gone?"

"Yes," he said grimly, "most of them managed to get into the boat. Don't be frightened. I think we're safer here than we should be with those ruffians."

Another man would have found easy terms of endearment and comfort for almost any woman so thrust on his protection and care, but the very depth of Coxeter's feeling seemed to make him dumb,—that and his anguished fear lest by his fault, by his own want of quickness, she had perhaps missed her chance of being saved.

But what he was lacking another man supplied. This was the captain, and Nan, listening to the cheering, commonplace words, felt her nerve, her courage, come back.

"Stayed with your husband?" he said, coming up to them. "Quite right, mum! Don't you be frightened. Look at me and my men, we're not frightened—not a bit of it! My boat will last right enough for us to be picked off ten times over. I tell you quite fairly and squarely, if I'd my wife aboard I'd 'a kept her with me. I'd rather be on this boat of mine than I would be out there, on the open water, in this fog." But as he walked back to the place where stood the rocket apparatus, Coxeter heard him mutter, "The brutes! Not all seconds or thirds either. I wish I had 'em here, I'd give 'em what for!"

Later, when reading the narratives supplied by some of the passengers who perforce had remained on the doomed boat, Coxeter was surprised to learn how many thrilling experiences he had apparently missed during the long four hours which elapsed before their rescue. And yet the time of waiting and suspense probably appeared as long to him as it did to any of the fifty odd souls who stayed, all close together, on the upper deck waiting with what seemed a stolid resignation for what might next befall them.

From the captain, Coxeter, leaving Mrs. Archdale for a moment, had extracted the truth. They had drifted down the French coast. They were on a dangerous reef of rock, and the rising of the wind, the lifting of the fog, for which they all looked so eagerly, might be the signal for the breaking up of the boat. On the other hand, the boat might hold for days. It was all a chance.

Coxeter kept what he had learnt to himself, but he was filled with a dull, aching sensation of suspense. His remorse that he had not hurried Mrs. Archdale into one of the first boats became almost intolerable. Why had he not placed her in the care even of the Jew, Victor Munich, who was actually seated in the last boat before the scramble round it had begun?

More fortunate than he, Mrs. Archdale found occupation in tending the few forlorn women who had been thrust back. He watched her moving among them with an admiration no longer unwilling; she looked bright, happy, almost gay, and the people to whom she talked, to whom she listened, caught something of her spirit. Coxeter would have liked to follow her example, but though he saw that some of the men round him were eager to talk and to discuss the situation, his tongue refused to form words of commonplace cheer.

When with the coming of the dawn the fog lifted, Nan came up to Coxeter as he stood apart, while the other passengers were crowding round a fire which had been lit on the open deck. Together in silence they watched the rolling away of the enshrouding mist; together they caught sight of the fleet of French fishing boats from which was to come succour.

As he turned and clasped her hand, he heard her say, more to herself than to him, "I did not think we should be saved."

III

John Coxeter was standing in the library of Mrs. Archdale's home in Wimpole Street. Two nights had elapsed since their arrival in London, and now he was to see her for the first time since they had parted on the Charing Cross platform, in the presence of the crowd of people comprised of unknown sympathisers, acquaintances, and friends who had come to meet them.

He looked round him with a curious sense of unfamiliarity. The colouring of the room was grey and white, with touches of deep-toned mahogany. It was Nan's favourite sitting-room, though it still looked what it had been ever since Nan could remember it—a man's room. In his day her father had been a collector of books, medals, and engravings connected with the severer type of eighteenth-century art and letters.

In a sense this room always pleased Coxeter's fancy, partly because it implied a great many things that money and even modern culture cannot buy. But now, this morning—for it was still early, and he was on his way to his office for the first time since what an aunt of his had called his mysterious preservation from death—he seemed to see everything in this room in another light. Everything which had once been to him important had become, if not worthless, then unessential.

He had sometimes secretly wondered why Mrs. Archdale, possessed as she was of considerable means, had not altered the old house, had not made it pretty as her friends' houses and rooms were pretty; but to-day he no longer wondered at this. His knowledge of the fleetingness of life, and of the unimportance of all he had once thought so important, was too vividly present. . . .

She came into the room, and he saw that she was dressed in a more feminine kind of garment than that in which he generally saw her. It was white, and though girdled with a black ribbon, it made her look very young, almost girlish.

For a moment they looked at one another in constraint. Mrs. Archdale also had altered, altered far less than John Coxeter, but she was aware, as he was not aware, of the changes which long nearness to death had brought her; and for almost the first time in her life she was more absorbed in her own sensations than in those of the person with her.

Seeing John Coxeter standing there waiting for her, looking so like his old self, so absolutely unchanged, confused her and made her feel desperately shy.

She held out her hand, but Coxeter scarcely touched it. After having held her so long in his arms, he did not care to take her hand in formal greeting. She mistook his gesture, thought that he was annoyed at having received no word from her since they had parted. The long day in between had been to Nan Archdale full of nervous horror, for relations, friends, acquaintances had come in troops to see her, and would not be denied.

Already she had received two or three angry notes from people who thought they loved her, and who were bitterly incensed that she had refused to see them when they had rushed to hear her account of an adventure which might so easily have happened to them. She made the mistake of confusing Coxeter with these selfish people.

"I am so sorry," she said in a low voice, "that when you called yesterday I was supposed to be asleep. I have been most anxious to see you"—she waited a moment and then added his name—"Mr. Coxeter. I knew that you would have the latest news, and that you would tell it me."

"There is news," he said, "of all the boats; good news—with the exception of the last boat——" His voice sounded strangely to himself.

"Oh, but that must be all right too, Mr. Coxeter! The captain said the boats might drift about for a long time."

Coxeter shook his head. "I'm afraid not," he said. "In fact"—he waited a moment, and she came close up to him.

"Tell me," she commanded in a low voice, "tell me what you know. They say I ought to put it all out of my mind, but I can think of nothing else. Whenever I close my eyes I see the awful struggle that went on round that last boat!" She gave a quick, convulsive sob.

Coxeter was dismayed. How wildly she spoke, how unlike herself she seemed to-day—

how unlike what she had been during the whole of their terrible ordeal.

Already that ordeal had become, to him, something to be treasured. There is no lack of physical courage in the breed of Englishmen to which John Coxeter belonged. Pain, entirely unassociated with shame, holds out comparatively little terror to such as he. There was something rueful in the look he gave her.

"The last boat was run down in the fog," he said briefly. "Some of the bodies have been washed up on the French coast."

She looked at him apprehensively. "Any of the people we had spoken to? Any of those who were with us in the railway carriage?"

"Yes, I'm sorry to say that one of the bodies washed up is that of the person who sat next to you."

"That poor French boy?"

Coxeter shook his head. "No, no—he's all right; at least I believe he's all right. It—the body I mean—was that of your other neighbour;" he added, unnecessarily, "the man who made sweets."

And then for the first time Coxeter saw Nan Archdale really moved out of herself. What he had just said had had the power to touch her, to cause her greater anguish than anything which had happened during the long hours of terror they had gone through. She turned and, moving as if blindly, pressed her hand to her face as if to shut out some terrible and pitiful sight.

"Ah!" she exclaimed in a low voice, "I shall never forgive myself over that! Do you know I had a kind of instinct that I ought to ask that man the name, the address"—her voice quivered and broke—"of his friend—of that poor young woman who saw him off at the Paris station."

Till this moment Coxeter had not known that Nan had been aware of what had, to himself, been so odious, so ridiculous, and so grotesque, a scene. But now he felt differently about this, as about everything else that touched on the quick of life. For the first time he understood, even sympathized with, Nan's concern for that majority of human beings who are born to suffering and who are bare to the storm. . . .

"Look here," he said awkwardly, "don't be unhappy. It's all right. That man spoke to me on the boat—he did what you wished, he made a will providing for that woman; I took charge of it for him. As a matter of fact I went and saw his old mother yesterday. She behaved splendidly."

"Then the life-saver was no good after all?'

"No good," he said, and he avoided looking at her. "At least so it would seem, but who can tell?"

Nan's eyes filled with tears; something beckoning, appealing seemed to pass from her to him. . . .

The door suddenly opened.

"Mrs. Eaton, ma'am. She says she only heard what happened, to-day, and she's sure you will see her."

Before Mrs. Archdale could answer, a woman had pushed her way past the maid into the room. "Nan? Poor darling! What an awful thing! I *am* glad I came so early; now you will be able to tell me all about it!"

The visitor, looking round her, saw John Coxeter, and seemed surprised. Fortunately she did not know him, and, feeling as if, had he stayed, he must have struck the woman, he escaped from the room.

As Coxeter went through the hall, filled with a perplexity and pain very alien from his positive nature, a good-looking, clean-shaven man, who gave him a quick measured glance, passed by. With him there had been no parleying at the door as in Coxeter's own case.

"Who's that?" he asked, with a scowl, of the servant.

"The doctor, sir," and he felt absurdly relieved. "We sent for him yesterday, for Mrs. Archdale seemed very bad last night." The servant dropped her voice, "It's the doctor, sir, as says Mrs. Archdale oughtn't to see visitors. You see it was in all the papers about the shipwreck, sir, and of course Mrs. Archdale's friends all come and see her to hear about it. They've never stopped. The doctor, he says that she ought to have stayed in bed and been quite quiet. But what would be the good of that, seeing she don't seem able to sleep? I suppose you've not suffered that way yourself, sir?"

The young woman was staring furtively at Coxeter, but, noting his cold manner and imperturbable face, she felt that he was indeed a disappointing hero of romance—not at all the sort of gentleman with whom one would care to be shipwrecked, if it came to a matter of choice.

"No," he said solemnly, "I can't say that I have."

He looked thoughtfully out into what had never been to him a "long unlovely street," and which just now was the only place in the world where he desired to stay. Coxeter, always so sure of himself, and of what was the best and wisest thing to do in every circumstance of life, felt for the first time unable to cope with a situation presented to his notice.

As he was hesitating, a carriage drove up, and a footman came forward with a card, while the occupant of the carriage called out, making anxious inquiries as to Mrs. Archdale's condition, and promising to call again the same afternoon.

Coxeter suddenly told himself that it behoved him to see the doctor, and ascertain from him whether Mrs. Archdale was really ill.

He crossed the street, and began pacing up and down, and unconsciously he quickened his steps as he went over every moment of his brief interview with Nan. All that was himself—and there was a good deal more of John Coxeter than even he was at all aware of—had gone out to her in a rapture of memory and longing, but she, or so it seemed to him, had purposely made herself remote.

At last, after what seemed a very long time, the doctor came out of Mrs. Archdale's house and began walking quickly down the street.

Coxeter crossed over and touched him on the arm. "If I may," he said, "I should like a word with you. I want to ask you—I mean I trust that Mrs. Archdale is recovering from the effect of the terrible experience she went through the other night." He spoke awkwardly, stiffly. "I saw her for a few minutes just before you came, and I was sorry to find her very unlike herself."

The doctor went on walking; he looked coldly at Coxeter.

"It's a great pity that Mrs. Archdale's friends can't leave her alone! As to being unlike herself, you and I would probably be very unlike ourselves if we had gone through what this poor lady had just gone through!"

"You see, I was with her on the boat. We were not travelling together," Coxeter corrected himself hastily, "I happened to meet her merely on the journey. My name is Coxeter."

The other man's manner entirely altered. He slackened in his quick walk. "I beg your pardon," he said; "of course I had no notion who you were. She says you saved her life! That but for you she would have been in that boat—the boat that was lost."

Coxeter tried to say something in denial of this surprising statement, but the doctor hurried on, "I may tell you that I'm very worried about Mrs. Archdale—in fact seriously concerned at her condition. If you have any influence with her, I beg you to persuade her to refuse herself to the endless busybodies who want to hear her account of what happened. She won't have a trained nurse, but there ought to be someone on guard—a human watchdog warranted to snarl and bite!"

"Do you think she ought to go away from London?" asked Coxeter in a low voice.

"No, I don't think that—at least not for the present," the medical man frowned thoughtfully. "What she wants is to be taken out of herself. If I could prescribe what I believe would be the best thing for her, I should advise that she go away to some other part of London with someone who will never speak to her of what happened, and yet who will always listen to her when she wants to talk about it—some sensible, commonplace person who could distract her mind without tiring her, and who would make her do things she has never done before. If she was an ordinary smart lady, I should prescribe philanthropy"—he made a slight grimace—"make her go and see some of my poorer patients—come into contact with a little *real* trouble. But that would be no change to Mrs. Archdale. No; what she wants is someone who will force her to be selfish—who will take her up the Monument one day, and to a music-hall the next, motor her out to Richmond Park, make her take a good long walk, and then sit by the sofa and hold her hand if she feels like crying——" He stopped, a little ashamed of his energy.

"Thank you," said Coxeter very seriously, "I'm much obliged to you for telling me this. I can see the sense of what you say."

"You know, in spite of her quiet manner, Mrs. Archdale's a nervous, sensitive woman"—the doctor was looking narrowly at Coxeter as he spoke.

"She was perfectly calm and—and very brave at the time——"

"That means nothing! Pluck's not a matter of nerve—it ought to be, but it isn't! But I admit you're a remarkable example of the presence of the one coupled with the absence of the other. You don't seem a penny the worse, and yet it must have been a very terrible experience."

"You see, it came at the end of my holiday," said Coxeter gravely, "and, as a matter of fact"—he hesitated—"I feel quite well, in fact, remarkably well. Do you see any objection to my calling again, I mean to-day, on Mrs. Archdale? I might put what you have just said before her."

"Yes, do! Do that by all means! Seeing how well you have come through it"—the doctor could not help smiling a slightly satirical smile—"ought to be a lesson to Mrs. Archdale. It ought to show her that after all she is perhaps making a great deal of fuss about nothing."

"Hardly that," said Coxeter with a frown.

They had now come to the corner of Queen Anne Street. He put out his hand hesitatingly. the doctor took it, and, oddly enough, held it for a moment while he spoke.

"Think over what I've said, Mr. Coxeter. It's a matter of hours. Mrs. Archdale ought to be taken in hand at once." Then he went off, crossing the street. "Pity the man's such a dry stick," he said to himself; "now's his chance, if he only knew it!"

John Coxeter walked straight on. He had written the day before to say that he would be at his office as usual this morning, but now the fact quite slipped his mind.

Wild thoughts were surging through his brain; they were running away with him and to such unexpected places!

The Monument? He had never thought of going up the Monument; he would formerly have thought it a sad waste of time, but now the Monument became to John Coxeter a place of pilgrimage, a spot of secret healing. A man had once told him that the best way to see the City was at night, but that if you were taking a lady you should choose a Sunday morning, and go there on the top of a 'bus. He had thought the man who said this very eccentric, but now he remembered the advice and thought it well worth following.

By the time Coxeter turned into Cavendish Square he had travelled far further than the Monument. He was in Richmond Park; Nan's hand was thrust through his arm, as it had been while they had watched the first boat fill slowly with the women and children.

To lovers who remember, the streets of a great town, far more than country roads and lanes, hold over the long years precious, poignant memories, for a background of stones and mortar has about it a character of permanence which holds captive and echoes the scenes and words enacted and uttered there.

Coxeter has not often occasion to go the little round he went that morning, but when some accidental circumstance causes him to do so, he finds himself again in the heart of that kingdom of romance from which he was so long an alien, and of which he has now become a naturalized subject. As most of us know, many ways lead to the kingdom of romance; Coxeter found his way there by a water-way.

And so it is that when he reaches the turning into Queen Anne Street there seems to rise round him the atmosphere of what Londoners call the City—the City as it is at night, uncannily deserted save for the ghosts and lovers who haunt its solitary thoroughfares after the bustle of the day is stilled. It was then that he and Nan first learnt to wander there. From there he travels on into golden sunlight; he is again in Richmond Park as it was during the whole of that beautiful October.

Walking up the west side of Cavendish Square, Coxeter again becomes absorbed in his great adventure,—a far greater adventure than that with which his friends and acquaintances still associate his name. With some surprise, even perhaps with some discomfiture, he sees himself—for he has not wholly cast out the old Adam —he sees himself as he was that memorable morning, carried, that is, wholly out of his usual wise, ponderate self. Perhaps he even wonders a little how he could ever have found courage to do what he did—he who has always thought so much, in a hidden way, of the world's opinion and of what people will say.

He could still tell you which lamp-post he was striding past when he realized, with a thrill of relief, that in any case Nan Archdale would not treat him as would almost certainly do one of those women whom he had honoured with his cold approval something less than a week ago. Any one of those women would have regarded what he was now going to ask

Nan to do as an outrage on the conventions of life. But Nan Archdale would be guided only by what she herself thought right and seemly. . . .

And then, as he turns again into Wimpole Street, as he comes near to what was once his wife's house, his long steady stride becomes slower. Unwillingly he is living again those doubtful moments when he knocked at her door, when he gave the surprised maid the confused explanation that he had a message from the doctor for Mrs. Archdale. He hears the young woman say, "Mrs. Archdale is just going out, sir. The doctor thought she ought to take a walk;" and his muttered answer, "I won't keep her a moment. . . ."

Again he feels the exultant, breathless thrill which seized him when she slipped, neither of them exactly knew how, into his arms, and when the sentences he had prepared, the arguments he meant to use, in his hurried rush up the long street, were all forgotten. He hears himself imploring her to come away with him now, at once. Is she not dressed to go out? Instinct teaches him for the first time to make to her the one appeal to which she ever responds. He had meant to tell her what the doctor had said—to let that explain his great temerity—but instead he tells her only that he wants her, that he cannot go on living apart from her. Is there any good reason why they should not start now, this moment, for Doctors' Commons, in order to see how soon they can be married?

So it is that when John-Coxeter stands in Wimpole Street, so typical a Londoner belonging to the leisured and conventional class that none of the people passing by even glance his way, he lives again through the immortal moment when she said, "Very well."

To this day, so transforming is the miracle of love, Nan Coxeter believes that during their curious honeymoon it was she who was taking care of John, not he of her.